WC CB   X

GW00602721

OP
7|11

Cold Spring Country

By the same author

The Sagebrush Sea
Guns of Revenge
Larkspur Range
Thunder Guns
Rebel Guns
Fast Guns of Deadwood
The Kansas Kid
Bitterbrush Range
Oxbow
The Pine Cone Ranch
Lee's Meadow Country
A Town Named Meridian
The Guns of Summer
The Expedition
Charley Choctaw
Sam Coyote
Strangers in Buckhorn
The Brass Bullet
The Overland Stage
The Last Ride
Garrison's Bounty
Fairchild

Cold Spring Country

JOHN HUNT

A Black Horse Western

ROBERT HALE · LONDON

© John Hunt 1997
First published in Great Britain 1997

ISBN 0 7090 6027 0

Robert Hale Limited
Clerkenwell House
Clerkenwell Green
London EC1R 0HT

Photoset in North Wales by
Derek Doyle & Associates, Mold, Flintshire.
Printed and bound in Great Britain by
WBC Book Manufacturers Limited,
Bridgend, Mid-Glamorgan.

1

The Circle W S Horses

It had been said of Abraham Carlyle that the Rocky Mountains had been a hole in the ground when he was born.

It was also said that he was by nature a hermit who avoided both the nearest settlement, Cold Spring, and human beings.

That he was as old as dirt was obvious, although he stood straight and was as lean as a cougar. His unshorn hair was white, his face was lined and weathered, his mouth lacked lips and he wore it in a straight line above his rock-set chin like a wound.

His eyes were faded blue and his hands were work-roughened. He had 2,000 deeded acres and woe to anyone he found trespassing. He rarely went without a Winchester saddle gun and absolutely never went without a holstered Colt slung from a shellbelt, things which did not set him entirely apart, but the big fleshing knife in a beaded scabbard had ceased to be common when the buffalo disappeared.

What was known about him derived from bits and

pieces, scraps of gossip, usually embellished. But one thing was undeniable; he had been in his foothill Rocky Mountain refuge since the oldest people in Cold Spring could recollect.

Two things contributed to his novelty: one was that when he came to the settlement for supplies he paid in raw gold, something which guaranteed gossip. The other thing was horses: he neither bought them nor raised them, he trapped them.

It was the gold that made bold spirits invade his land. They came in the springtime, during summer and into autumn, and rarely did their spying and digging go undetected.

He was so good at catching trespassers it was said he had eyes in the back of his head, and there was something else; when he caught them he made them take off their pants and underpants. Apprehended trespassers commonly waited until the darkness of night to sneak back into the settlement.

By any measurement Abraham Carlyle would not have won a popularity contest. Stretching it a bit further, neither would he have won a beauty pageant because, although he had been a ruggedly handsome man in his prime, age had changed that.

Among the rumours around Cold Spring was one that forty or fifty years earlier he'd had a woman, sometimes said to have been a Shoshone. Other times said to have been a Mandan. The only old-timers who might have been able to verify that had been dead a long time, which did not ameliorate the story.

Cold Spring was what had been called 'a well and a peach tree at the side of the roads'. That description still fitted the place. Once there had been an army post east of the settlement, but it had disappeared piecemeal after the soldiers left, windows and doors, roof baulks and iron had been incorporated into the village.

Cold Spring had a saloon owned by a man named Josiah Parker. It also had a Baptist church at the north end of the village. Because Cold Spring had been a freighters' haven for years there was also a smithy, a café and a log jailhouse inside of which bored guests had carved names, initials and dates.

The jailhouse had once been a Christian mission, but that hadn't lasted long; hunters, explorers, freighters and a variety of rough frontiersmen had avoided the church as often as they had avoided the log *cárcel* which consisted of one room with narrow barred windows and an old table where a constable presided. He also served as the village justice – when there was a constable in Cold Spring.

Cold Spring was a good sixty miles from the nearest town, which lay south-east and was called Glorioso, for what reason no one knew because the Glorioso countryside was barren of timber, had immense boulders and consisted mostly of ancient adobe buildings. Glorioso was supported by a military post called Fort Buchanan, locally referred to as Fort Mud because the buildings inside the stockade were adobe and had once housed Mexican soldiers; that was before the US-Mexican war when, at the Treaty of Guadalupe Hidalgo, Mexico had lost all of her westerly territories, which was nothing of great moment; nine tenths of *Mejico*'s inhabitants had no idea concerning the extent of their country, certainly they had no idea about the parched south-west.

Fort Buchanan housed *norteamericano soldados* and

had since most folks could remember.

Cold Spring had no such source of economic security. Even the freight road was a mile west of the settlement, but freighters used Cold Spring's network of pole corrals for the same reason people lived in Cold Spring. It was in the name: there was a large cold-water spring at the middle of the settlement which generations of people had with almost religious concern encircled with an adobe wall about waist high to prevent children, small animals and large ones from falling in.

Water was everything in the Glorioso territory, which was a semi-desert area. Sixty miles north of Cold Spring there was no water problem and the land was rich in grass, browse and in Abraham Carlyle's area, immense stands of timber.

The sardonic, lanky man named Arch Trumbull, who not only owned a general store in Cold Spring but who also acted as constable and justice, had often said the difference between the north country and the south country was the difference between heaven and purgatory.

Something else the turkey-necked, tall constable said in his dry manner, was that Abraham Carlyle knew the heavily timbered and rugged uplands better than the Indians had. How Arch Trumbull knew this he did not explain nor was he the kind of person who took kindly to being questioned.

A grizzled stockman who operated a cattle outfit south-west of Cold Spring, whose name was Timothy Farrel, a widower without issue who had prospered over the years because after the passing of his wife he had devoted every waking hour to his livestock business, and because he was shrewd, had prospered. He and the constable had a few things in common. Neither was talkative, both were tall, lean individuals and between the pair of them they had managed their territory without any more than the usual amount of difficulty.

At least this had obtained until a stranger named Will Stanton appeared in Cold Spring one summer morning, went to the general store in search of Arch Trumbull and asked if the constable-justice knew a man named Abraham Carlyle. When the constable nodded the burly, greying, weathered and faded stranger said, 'I run stock fifteen, twenty miles north, beyond the mountains, an' I come up shy ten of my using horses, an' I tracked 'em through the mountains, found 'em in a corral a few yards from a log house with the name Abraham Carlyle carved in the door.'

Arch Trumbull considered the stockman in silence for a moment before saying, 'You didn't meet him, did you?'

'There wasn't no one around.'

Trumbull almost imperceptibly inclined his head. 'I figured you didn't meet him because you got your pants on.'

Will Stanton stared. Arch did not explain about Abraham Carlyle's unique punishment for trespassers. Instead he said, 'I expect you'd know your own horses, friend, but I've known that old man close to twenty years an' I never before even heard a rumour that he'd steal horses.'

The burly man was unimpressed. 'I'd take it kindly if you bein' the local lawman would ride up there with me. Them horses is branded on the left shoulder with the letters W S in a circle.'

Arch Trumbull considered the stockman for a moment before speaking again. 'I can't just lock up the store, an' that's a considerable distance, Mister Stanton.'

The greying, husky man narrowed his eyes slightly and cocked his head. 'Friend, them horses was the best animals in my string of workin' animals.' Stanton paused, still with his head slightly cocked. 'They was stole out of my corral in the night. By the time I went lookin' for them they was up in the wild country, but trackin' ten barefoot horses isn't hard. Especially the thief's animal. It was shod an' left marks wherever it crossed rock fields.'

Arch Trumbull went into another of his laconic and lengthy silences before speaking again. 'I'll lock up an' ride with you, but I should tell you Abraham Carlyle don't take at all kindly to trespassers, 'specially one like you who is a stranger.'

Stanton was still unimpressed. Before heading for the door he asked where he could hire a fresh animal; the one he'd ridden was tuckered.

Trumbull told him to try the settlement black-smith who horse-traded in his spare time, and watched the burly man leave his store.

The constable-justice was not enthusiastic about the long ride nor the welcome at the other end. He knew Abe Carlyle better than most folks, but it couldn't be said they were friends. As far as Trumbull knew Carlyle had no friends.

What had aroused his interest was the statement Stanton had made about tracking a horsethief who rode a shod horse. Abe Carlyle never shod his saddle animals. He had enough so that when one got tender he'd turn it out and bring in another one.

The holy man, in the act of whitewashing the church, watched them ride north and waved. Arch Trumbull waved back. He was not a member of the reverend's flock but they were friends of long standing.

On the ride, made mostly in silence, Trumbull cryptically told the stockman what he knew about Abraham Carlyle. He stopped when he recognized the rock-set of Will Stanton's jaw. The man from up north was obviously a person whose interest was habitually fixed on one thing at a time, and right now, as they rode without haste through a beautiful sunbright day, he was only interested in recovering his animals.

Arch Trumbull could not fault that. In Stanton's boots he would have reacted pretty much in the same way. But as they got closer to the forbidding uplands where sunlight rarely reached, he squinted ahead. According to local gossip no one ever sneaked up on Abe Carlyle. Arch sighed to himself. They were the only moving objects across miles of open country under a dazzlingly bright sun; if the old man was up there he would know they were coming, and he would not have to climb higher into the foothills behind his yard to know that.

An ancient pair of wagon ruts made a circuitous path to the weathered log house with its magnificent spread of elk antlers over the door.

The constable hesitated before dismounting. The pole corrals were empty except for something shy of a dozen horses lined up like crows on a fence watching Trumbull and his companion. There was not a sound, the stovepipe had no smoke showing. Old Carlyle had once had a large black dog but he'd died some years back.

As they dismounted and Stanton looped his reins through an iron stud ring in the front wall, the tall, laconic man from Cold Spring spoke so softly it seemed he was addressing himself.

'It don't feel right,' he said, and his spurs jingled as he went to a low-roofed log barn as old and weathered as the house. Stanton trailed him. He too seemed to feel uncomfortable.

Inside the empty barn Stanton said, 'You don't expect the damned horsethief's out yonder with a rifle do you?'

Arch turned irritably. 'If he's a horsethief, Mister Stanton, I'm the Angel Gabriel.' Trumbull went to the doorless barn opening and stood gazing in as many directions as he could see. When Stanton came up Trumbull said, 'Something's wrong.'

Stanton said nothing.

A corralled horse nickered, they went over there and found the leaky old stone trough bone dry. They found the small hollow log which ran up into the northward low swales, unplugged it with a wire and watched the renewed flow of water. They had to stop several horse fights as the animals crowded to drink.

The constable stood in thought for a while. From what he knew of Abraham Carlyle he cared for horses, all animals. He would never have allowed that trough to go empty if he could have prevented it.

Stanton broke across Trumbull's reverie when he said, 'That leggy seal brown is my top cuttin' horse.' Stanton leaned on a corral stringer. 'Two years back I turned down an offer of a hunnert dollars for that horse.'

Trumbull also leaned on a peeled log stringer.

'Good animals,' he said quietly, and added a little more. 'The old man traps wild horses. Look at these corrals, posts set at six feet apart, topmost stringers better'n five feet.'

Stanton watched his horses drink. 'How many horses does he have?'

The constable had no idea; for that matter no one else would have any idea, but the constable said, 'He's likely out settin' up a trap.'

Stanton made a dry comment about that. 'Or maybe crossin' the mountains to steal horses.'

Arch turned on the husky man. 'You got a pigheaded streak, Mister Stanton,' and the stockman, stung, answered curtly. 'Those are my horses in his corral. How do you explain that?'

Trumbull looked steadily at the other man. 'I'll tell you how I explain it: you tracked your horsethief ridin' a shod horse.'

Stanton nodded without speaking.

'Abe Carlyle never shod his horses. He didn't have to; when one got tender he'd turn it out and use another one, but he doesn't shoe his horses.'

Stanton looked in at the horses and said nothing until they were moving away. They were near the log house when he spoke again. 'Where is he? He could clear this up. How long we got to set here until he comes back?'

Trumbull was reaching for the latch string when he replied, 'As long as it takes.'

'Constable, I got work to do at home. You saw their brands. They're my animals. I can drive them back where they come from an' when you find Carlyle you can find out how my horses come to be in his corral.'

The door opened easily. Inside, there was one

large room. An iron stove stood in one corner with cooking pans suspended from antlers nearby.

The bed was wide and long, and hadn't been made in a long time. Stanton sniffed. 'Typical boar's nest,' he said, gazing at a Winchester rifle in a gloomy corner. On a peg close to the bed a worn old shellbelt with a holstered six-gun was suspended from a wall peg.

While the constable was by the stove Stanton approached the bed and stopped stone still. In a quiet voice he said, 'Constable. . . ?'

Arch saw the dried blood and turned slowly looking for a trail of drops. They were difficult to distinguish because the wooden flooring was dark and stained with age.

2

Riding in the Wrong Direction

They hadn't paid attention to the yard out front but now they did. There were no distinguishable drops of blood but there was something which meant nothing to Stanton but which meant a lot to the constable.

He stared at the ground as he quietly said, 'The old man's got big feet,' and pointed. 'Those tracks wasn't made by him, they're too small. And look there, someone made them tracks wearin' spurs with big rowels. The old man never used spurs. I doubt if he even owned a pair.'

Stanton frowned as he started walking parallel to the boot prints. They led to an old log shed about the size of a storehouse. At the sturdy handmade door Stanton stepped aside.

The constable pushed the door open. Stale air came out. The shed had no windows just the door. It was dark inside until the door was opened.

Arch Trumbull stood in the doorway without moving. He said, 'There he is,' and moved clear so the stockman could also enter.

Stanton stiffened. 'He's been here a while.'

Trumbull nodded absently without going any closer. Lying nearby was the shaft for either an axe or a splitting wedge. Despite the dark coolness of the shed blood on the shaft was dry and dark.

Stanton said, 'Hit him twice, once at the house and finished the job in here.' Stanton went closer and leaned. Abraham Carlyle had been propped against the wall. Stanton said, 'Been dead some time, Constable,' and Trumbull nodded.

Stanton straightened up. 'Pockets been turned inside out. He either knew who killed him or got snuck up on, wouldn't you say?'

The constable did not reply, he went back out into the sunshine. He and Abraham Carlyle hadn't been friends, at least not in the way folks meant when they spoke of friends, but they had spoken a few times. Once the old recluse had invited the constable to ride up and see him some time, something Arch Trumbull had never done and now wished he had.

Stanton left the shed and closed the door. He studied the house. 'I expect a man who lives alone an' apart's got to figure someday he'd wish he had neighbours,' he said.

Trumbull returned to the house. Stanton went to the corral where his horses had tanked up and were now hungry. Inside the barn he found a three-tined hay fork, a loft half full of timothy and forked feed down into the corral. While he was up there he saw movement among the big northward stands of timber, leaned on the fork in the loft door watching. He was motionless and in shadows.

It was two horsemen. They sat still in a piece of stump land where the sun reached. They were clearly watching the Carlyle yard.

Stanton left the fork in the loft, climbed down and by keeping the barn between himself and the strangers reached the cabin as the constable appeared in the doorway on his way. Stanton pushed him back, told Trumbull what he had seen and the constable nodded. 'Two of 'em? Where's the other one been hidin' out?'

Stanton cracked the door slightly to peek out. The particular place he had seen the riders could not be seen from the doorway so he stepped outside and the constable spoke sharply to him.

'Get back in here! They've seen our horses an' know there's two of us.' When the stockman was back inside the constable also said, 'This is bushwhackin' country. If we stay in here they got to come to us. If they come.'

But they didn't come. After an hour Stanton and the constable left the house doing their best to use shadows and buildings for cover. They spent more than another hour trying to at least get a sighting of the horsemen before giving up.

The day was dying. It was a long ride back to the settlement, they killed time caring for their mounts in the barn while solid shadows lengthened. When they were ready to leave, although neither man spoke, their thoughts were identical.

Darkness came early in the highlands which wasn't much consolation, and they used every ruse they knew while silently sharing a conviction that if those illusive horsemen intended to ambush them there was precious little they could do about it that they weren't doing.

Two miles south-east in the direction of the settlement Stanton sounded relieved when he said, 'They come from the north. There's some almighty rugged country up there, I know that for a fact because I come down here that way. Constable, I'd like to hire some men to help me drive my horses home.'

Arch Trumbull dryly said, 'Use the stage road, an' you better hire real good men. Every mile of that road's got trees right down to the berm.' After a moment of silence the constable also said, 'Those are good animals, Mister Stanton. I wonder if the best horses on earth are worth gettin' shot in the back over.'

Cold Spring's lights showed with the passing of dusk. They parted out front of Arch Trumbull's store, Arch went inside, the stockman led his hired horse down to the corral behind the smithy.

The waspish widow-woman who clerked at the store scowled at the constable. 'I was fixin' to lock up for the night. My belly thinks my throat's been cut.' She stamped out of the store and Trumbull locked the door behind her, took a lamp to his lean-to living-quarters out back, hung the light from a ceiling wire and sprawled in a chair.

Someone had to go back up yonder and bury Abraham Carlyle. The idea of being away from his store for so long and so often was annoying. On the other hand, whoever Stanton had seen up there, just might bury the old man. But it wasn't likely.

Trumbull got to his feet, fired up the stove, drank briefly from a bottle and started making supper. No one was going to bury the old man, certainly not whoever had killed him, and certainly no one from the settlement who didn't know he was dead and, furthermore, hadn't cared much for him.

And that left Constable Trumbull. He had buried folks before, but in designated graveyards, not up north where he wasn't even sure the old man'd have digging tools.

And – if Will Stanton hired a small posse to go back for his horses and drive them home – Arch took two more swallows from the bottle – as sure as Gawd had made green grass he wasn't going to find any horses.

He bedded down accompanied by some unpleasant thoughts. For as long as he'd been in the Cold Spring country, something like sixteen, eighteen years, he'd never been required to solve a murder nor run down horsethieves.

The settlement was a peaceful, drowsy place; people knew everyone else's business, scraped out a living and while there were dissidents, such as the rangemen who worked for the outlying ranches, between the constable and Josiah Parker the saloon-man who kept an ash wagon spoke on a shelf below his bar, order was kept.

He was awakened by a chorus of town dogs raising Cain and propping him up. Because there was an alley door but no window in his living area the constable had to stamp into his boots and go through the dark store to see the roadway from a glass window.

The settlement was dark and the roadway was empty. He was about to go back to bed when he detected the sound of distant animals running. There was even a slight reverberation in the store's floor.

It was too early for the stockmen to be making a drive down to the railroad pens at Glorioso, nor did it sound like cattle. If it was cattle their owner was either crazy or had a stampede on his hands. The best way to shrink saleable livestock was to allow them to run.

He unlocked the door and stepped out onto the plankwalk. It wasn't cattle, it was horses, a lot of horses, and they were hightailing it southward. Once he thought he heard a man shout but wasn't sure, the distance was too great and running horses drowned out just about all other sounds.

There was no moon so it had to be very late, possibly two or three o'clock in the morning. He went back inside to get dressed. By the time he returned to the roadway the sound was less than a whisper. Several lights appeared and someone growled his name from the lower end of the settlement. He met the horse-trading blacksmith midway and Meeker said, 'What in the hell was that?'

Trumbull answered laconically. 'Horses.'

'In the middle of the gawddamned night?'

'A big herd of them. How come they woke you up, Jim?'

'Sounded like a train. Shook my bed. I been a light sleeper since In'ians snuck up on me and liked to have lifted my hair twenty years ago. Whose horses, Arch, an' why drive 'em in the dark? Best way on earth to lose some of 'em.'

The constable did not reply. On his way back to the store he thought about saddling up and going after the horses. The reason he didn't was because, summer or not, the predawn morning was chilly. He couldn't have overtaken them anyway. His last thought before going back to sleep had to do with the question of so many horses and why they had been close enough to Cold Spring to rattle windows.

In the morning he was frying breakfast when someone insistently rattled the roadway door. He dried both hands and went up front.

The insistent knocker was Will Stanton. He pushed in as he said, 'I met the preacher at the café a while ago. He said a band of In'ians drivin' a hunnert horses run past last night.'

The constable showed neither any expression nor interest as he said, 'You want some breakfast?' With his back to the stockman he led the way to his living-quarters where frying meat and spuds were curling.

Stanton sat on a bench, watched the constable work to salvage his breakfast and would have spoken if Arch hadn't turned with his breakfast on a chipped platter as he said, 'There's been no In'ians in this country for thirty years, an' if there was where would they get a big band of horses?' As he finished speaking the constable sat at his table staring wide-eyed at the stockman.

Stanton said, 'What?'

'The old man's horses.'

'Carlyle?'

'No one else had that many horses. He trapped 'em, gentled 'em and hardly ever sold a single one.'

'How many did he have?'

'You asked me that yesterday. I don't know. I doubt that maybe he even knew. I'd guess he had as many as went south last night.'

Stanton said, 'Eat before it gets cold.'

As the constable went to work on his platter he jerked his head. 'There's coffee on the stove.'

Will Stanton got a cupful, returned to the bench, sat down and raised the cup to his mouth. He suddenly put the cup down. Arch Trumbull said, 'It takes real men to drink my coffee.'

Stanton scowled. 'You could sell that stuff to an embalmer.'

The constable replied around a mouthful of fried meat. 'I was raised up hard, we never wasted anythin'. My mother said waste was a sin.' He swallowed and speared another piece of meat. 'I add more grounds when the water gets low. Don't throw the grounds away until the coffee gets a puny colour.'

Stanton ignored both the cup on the bench at his side and the pot on the stove. 'If they was Carlyle's horses mine could have been among 'em.'

Trumbull discreetly raised a hand to muffle the noise and belched, then he said, 'Likely. I'm goin' back up there an' bury the old man. If you come along we'll find out whether your horses was in that drive. The ground up there'll be hard, I could use some help.'

Stanton had already spent more time in the Cold Spring country than he had anticipated. He had a wife and two sons who would look after things but, as he said, running down those horses might take days, which was something he would not do with pleasure.

Trumbull's reply was curt. 'You want your horses back you won't do it settin' in here nor goin' home.'

They rigged out in silence and said little until a mile or so west they came upon the tracks of a sizeable herd of barefoot horses being driven south.

They changed course and rode in the wake of the horse herd. As long as it was cool they made good time but when heat came into the morning they slackened off. As Trumbull said, if they continued in the southerly direction they would eventually pass the village of Glorioso. He had to explain what and where the southerly town was and Stanton seemed to absorb this information without enthusiasm. The further they went south the further he was getting from home.

Driving horses at the rate those animals had been driven in the night invariably resulted in a few head being either overlooked in the darkness or deliberately abandoned for several reasons, one of which was age, another was mares heavy with foals.

About halfway between Cold Spring and Glorioso they encountered their first animal – it was a rawboned big bay gelding with a flat chin and sunken eyes surrounded by grey hair. He was standing near some huge rocks and barely acknowledged the approach of riders. He wasn't breathing hard but was clearly exhausted, too tired even to sidle clear of horsemen. He looked at them with a dull-eyed gaze. Stanton said, 'Plumb tuckered an' dang near as old as I am.'

Trumbull sat gazing at the old horse. He recognized him; on the rare occasions old Carlyle had appeared in town for supplies, the old pelter was the animal between the shafts of Carlyle's buggy.

Some distance on southward they found two more animals, two heavy mares and both as worn down as the old buggy animal had been except that their reason for not being with the drive had less to do with age than it had to do with the extra weight they were carrying, and the mares moved warily away as the riders approached. They had recovered from their ordeal and being young their recovery was faster.

Trumbull knew neither of the mares which made

little difference, dried sweat made it clear that they had belonged to the drive.

They made no attempt to get close. Stanton said, 'Would they be headin' for that town you mentioned?'

'Glorioso? I'd guess they'd bypass it the same as they did Cold Spring.' He also said, 'Somewhere they had to slack off. Messicans won't buy wind-broke animals.'

'How far's the border beyond Glorioso?' Stanton asked, and got a laconic reply. 'Too far for horses to be run the way those animals is bein' pushed. About eight, ten miles.'

'You reckon they'd be Messicans?'

Trumbull paused in the feeble speckled shade of a paloverde tree when he answered. 'I got no idea. If we keep on the trail we're goin' to have to ride the rest of today, tonight an' tomorrow, an' by now they're over the line down into Messico.' Trumbull paused briefly before saying the rest of it. 'Mister Stanton, no one recovers horses or cattle once they cross the border. If you want to try, go right ahead, but I can tell you somethin' about that: even if the horsethieves don't shoot you the villagers'll steal your horse'n outfit an' cut your throat for your boots. Me; I've seen enough. I'm goin' back.'

Stanton rode back the way they had come in silence. He had no way of knowing whether his horses were among the animals in the drive, but only an incurable optimist would have thought otherwise.

He asked questions about the Glorioso country-side. He also asked about old man Carlyle and his segment of the area.

Trumbull answered as best he could. When he

could not answer a question he simply said nothing.

By the time they had Cold Spring in sight the sun had been high for a long time and even as it slanted off westerly the heat lingered. The men were hungry; their mounts were more thirsty than hungry.

It was dusk when they rode into the settlement, there were few people in sight but the horse-trading blacksmith had a lighted lantern hanging in his sooty place of business and said little as Will Stanton returned the hired animal and paid for its use. As he and Arch Trumbull were leaving the blacksmith said, 'If you don't want to get ragged to death don't go to the saloon. Everyone's fired up about a ghost herd of horses passin' last night.'

They didn't go to the saloon, they went to the café which, fortunately, was empty except for the proprietor who had been reading a dogeared newspaper when they walked in and, as was his custom, folded the paper slowly, gazed stonily at the tired-looking, dusty men and said, 'Beef stew, mashed potatoes an' coffee.'

Trumbull sat down as he nodded. When the café-man had gone to his kitchen Trumbull laconically said, 'He's got a disposition like a bear with a sore behind an' can't cook worth a damn, but he's all we got.'

As Stanton was eating he made a statement. 'I'm goin' to ride up to the Carlyle place in the mornin' an' if my horses are there, I'm goin' to drive 'em home.'

The lanky man at Stanton's side made no comment until he'd swallowed, then all he said was, 'Your horses won't be up there, but I'll keep you company with a wagon. The old man's got to be buried.' Trumbull wiped up gravy with a piece of bread before finishing it. 'Old Abraham's got to be buried soon; the weather's stayin' warm.'

As they were leaving the eatery to go out into moonless darkness Trumbull paused at sucking his teeth to ask a question. 'If your horses aren't up there, just how are you goin' to get home? It'll be one hell of a long walk.'

Stanton made no reply. He considered the lighted saloon but when they parted he went south not north, down where behind the smithy there was a large shock of hay. A man could do a lot worse in a place where there was no overnight public accommodation.

Arch Trumbull went through the store to his living-quarters and found a note propped against the cold coffee pot atop the stove.

It wasn't signed and had been obviously written very laboriously. He would have recognized the handwriting blindfolded. The cranky woman who minded the store in his absence had written the note.

It informed him that an army officer had come to the store asking directions to the Carlyle's place. He had said the old hermit had contracted to supply the garrison down near Glorioso with forty head of horses.

Arch stood a long time gazing at the note. In the first place he knew for a fact from one of his visits to the old man that Carlyle never sold his horses. He also knew the old man couldn't have signed a contract with the army or anyone else because he could neither read nor write.

He pocketed the note and retired, but sleep was a long time coming. Hindsight being better than foresight he let go a noisy long sigh: He should have gone north as he'd originally intended, not south, on the day which was now ending.

In the morning after filling up at the eatery he went to the smithy where the blacksmith told him Will Stanton had hired an animal about an hour earlier and had left town riding northward.

The blacksmith loaned him a light wagon, tossed in digging tools, backed a harness horse between the shafts and leaned in the doorway of his smithy watching Trumbull drive north out of Cold Spring using the north-south stage road.

The horse-trading blacksmith, whose name was Jim Meeker, was still leaning there in new-day warmth when Tim Farrel, the cowman from northwest of Cold Spring, arrived on a good-looking chestnut sorrel gelding whose feet were four inches too long.

Farrel left the animal to be shod and went in the direction of the café. For him, it had been a long, chilly ride. He could have sent one of his riders, of whom he kept two, year round. The reason he hadn't was because he hadn't picked up the mail in about a month, and also because he had a hankering for the local seamstress, Mary Elkins, the same testy widow-woman who clerked at Trumbull's store.

Their relationship was not dissimilar to that of a wasp and a honey bee. It had been said around the settlement that when a lifelong bachelor was in the rut and choices were very limited, he would likely settle for anything that squatted to pee.

3
Found Horses

The constable didn't overtake the stockman. Stanton saw him coming and dismounted in tree shade to wait. Where they met each man nodded, Stanton got back astride and they exchanged no words until they had old Abraham's log house in sight, then Stanton spoke of something Trumbull had already noticed.

'There's a soldier watchin' us from the doorway.'

Arch hadn't expected the soldier to still be there. When they were close the townsmen waved and the blue-belly waved back. Where they tied up out front of the barn the soldier, a grizzled sergeant built like a brick outhouse, came over and said, 'Did you gents know the old man?'

Trumbull nodded. 'I did.'

'He's in the shed deader'n a door nail.'

When they had cared for their animals the sergeant introduced himself as Tom Fitzpatrick, sergeant, stationed at Fort Buchanan near Glorioso. Arch introduced himself and Will Stanton, then took digging tools from the wagon bed and said, 'We come to look for horses an' bury the old man.'

The sergeant watched Arch unload the tools and

asked if Trumbull knew what had happened to the old man. Arch dryly replied, 'Got killed by an axe handle.'

'Who did it?' Fitzpatrick asked, and got a dispassionate gaze from the Cold Spring constable. 'I got no idea.'

Will Stanton called from the corrals. 'They're gone. The thievin' sons of bitches got my horses.'

Sergeant Fitzpatrick frowned. 'What's he yellin' about?'

'He had ten of his horses in the corral. They was stole from him some time back. He's got a cow outfit on the far side of the mountains.'

Fitzpatrick returned his attention to Trumbull as he produced a wrinkled piece of paper, smoothed it and said, 'Mister Carlyle agreed to sell the army forty horses an' deliver 'em better'n a week ago. This here is his signed agreement.'

Arch ignored the paper when he said, 'He didn't sign no paper, Sergeant.'

Fitzpatrick reddened. 'That's his signature!'

Arch still ignored the paper. 'Sergeant, old Abraham couldn't read nor write.'

Fitzpatrick was not surprised. He held out the contract. 'Then who signed this?'

Arch didn't answer the question, he asked one of his own. 'When did you leave the fort?'

'Four days ago. Why?'

'Because I think your forty horses was delivered at Fort Buchanan a couple of days ago. They sure was drove in that direction.'

Fitzpatrick let the hand fall to his side with the contract in it. 'Are you sure?' he asked.

'Nope, I'm not sure, but if your paymaster had the

money to pay I'd say the horses was delivered. A band of horses was drove south toward Glorioso a couple of nights back. Until we met I figured whoever drove 'em was headin' for Messico, but now I don't think Messico was their destination.'

Will Stanton came from the corral wiping sweat off his white forehead. He dropped his hat back down and ignored the soldier to glare at the constable. 'I want them horses back,' he exclaimed. 'If I got to dog 'em to Hell an' for two days over the coals.'

Arch handed Stanton and the soldier a shovel, took a pick and a crowbar himself and looked around as he said, 'By that old cottonwood tree.' His selection of the site of the grave was motivated by cottonwood shade and nothing else.

Sergeant Fitzpatrick was a powerful man. He talked as he worked. Will Stanton, on the other hand, although accustomed to manual labour, did not say ten words during the hours required for the grave to be dug to a depth of slightly over four feet, and had its vertical sides evened up.

They went to the cabin where it was cool, drank from Abraham's water gourd, and rested. The sergeant told Arch Trumbull that if the constable was right, then he'd made one hell of a long ride for nothing.

Will Stanton sourly said, 'If you'd get telegraph wires strung over here all you'd have to do would be to telegraph that fort.'

Fitzpatrick eyed the stockman dispassionately. 'Friend, if cows could fly folks'd have to wear iron hats.'

The most unpleasant part was rolling Carlyle into a blanket, he'd been dead a fair length of time.

They lowered him into the grave and went to work filling it in. The sergeant was leaning on a shovel when he asked if Carlyle kept a jug somewhere about.

Arch had no answer and Will Stanton simply shrugged. He had never been much of a drinking man and right now his second foremost concern was eating.

The sun was reddening off toward the highest part of the northerly primitive country when Arch patted and mounded the grave. He told himself that some-day he'd come up here and put a decent marker over it.

They returned to the house where Arch rummaged for what was available and made a meal. Before they had finished Arch had to light a lantern.

Sergeant Fitzpatrick dug out an ugly little pipe, stuffed it with shag and leaned above the lamp mantle to get the thing going.

To men who did not smoke the aroma was just short of overwhelming. Will Stanton cracked the door and, not too distant, a wolf sat back and sounded.

Fitzpatrick said he would return to Fort Buchanan and Will Stanton immediately said he would accom-pany the soldier. Fitzpatrick nodded and asked if the Stanton horses had been branded.

Stanton drew a fingernail sketch on the table top as he replied. 'Left shoulder.' The sergeant removed his pipe long enough to consider the scratching, leaned back and said, 'Mister, if your ten head make up the forty, why I expect the army'll pay you for 'em.'

Arch knew what that remark would cause and he

was right. The cowman looked steadily at the old campaigner when he said, 'Those horses aren't for sale.'

The burly Irishman plugged his pipe back into place, eyed the stockman and said nothing.

When they prepared to bed down after caring for their horses, Arch thought he might ride to the fort too. He also thought he could discern the vague shape of an idea he did not like; involvement in a complicated plot that meant someone who was very coyote had hatched, and in so doing had dragged the constable into it up to his gullet.

Before closing his eyes wrapped in a smelly old blanket on the floor, a thought arrived that increased his anxiety: whoever had stolen the horses had to be the same person who had signed that contract with the army, and that meant this had not been a simple matter of horsethieves killing an old man, rounding up his horses and stampeding them southward in the night.

He had never before since arriving in the Cold Spring country and opening his store, felt anything but satisfaction the way fate, or someone anyway, had ordered his life. As he drifted off to sleep he felt different.

In the morning while the others were getting ready to ride, Arch returned to the cabin for old Abraham's guns and shellbelt and made a startling discovery.

Tucked under two folded blankets on a shelf was a pair of moccasins, too small for a man, certainly a man with feet as large as Abraham's feet had been.

They were not quite new but hadn't been worn much. The old man hadn't made them, his large hands and thick fingers never could have managed that kind of sewing with gut, but what kept the constable motionless were the beaded initials M.C.

Trumbull's first impression was that they had belonged to an Indian woman rumour said Abraham had shared his log house with many years earlier, but when he turned them over he found dried earth, which had to mean the moccasins had probably been worn no later than the previous winter.

He put them back beneath the blankets, returned to the yard and, leaving the wagon, mounted his horse and rode with his companions in complete silence.

Sergeant Fitzpatrick had questions. Because of the constable's silence Will Stanton had to answer them as best he could, but there was more he didn't know than he did know, so eventually, when they were halfway along, the sergeant eased up beside the constable and asked if Arch felt all right. He got a nod but no words.

Being by nature as well as by training, a blunt individual, the soldier said, 'What's botherin' you, Constable?' and this time he got an answer.

'If the old man's horses is in the corral at Fort Buchanan,' he said, 'that'll explain somethin' an' I expect the army'll have got a bill of sale, an' maybe that'll end the army's concern, but it leaves me with a lot of questions.'

The sergeant was sympathetic. 'About the old man? Constable, it happens every day, folks get killed.' The sergeant shrugged thick shoulders. 'You'll sort it out. You know the people an' the country an' you got the time.'

Trumbull said no more until they had Glorioso in

sight, then he loped ahead watching the sign of many driven horses.

He had felt certain the thieves had headed straight for Mexico, but they hadn't; their trail cut south easterly below the village. Sergeant Fitzpatrick loped ahead. When he was gone Will Stanton came up and said, 'Bill of sale or no bill of sale my horses are branded. It's a registered brand an' without my signature on a bill of sale, the army can't keep 'em.'

Arch watched the palisade gates swing open. Several soldiers with saddle guns came out. When the pair of civilian riders passed through, Stanton raised a hand and the soldiers returned the gesture.

Sergeant Fitzpatrick was waiting on the porch of the command hut. Beside him was a fine-boned, shorter man with the insignia of a major on his shoulders. He had sharp features and steady dark eyes.

When Arch and the stockman swung off and tied up, the major introduced himself. 'Frank Maxwell, Major commanding.'

The major did not offer his hand, he led the way inside his command post, gestured toward chairs and leaned on his desk as he said, 'Sergeant Fitzpatrick has told me about the horses. Gentlemen, we have them and we have a bill of sale.'

Arch had a question. 'Who signed it, Major?'

'Abraham Carlyle.'

Arch gently wagged his head. 'Abraham Carlyle couldn't have signed it. He was dead, an' he also couldn't read nor write.'

Will Stanton broke in, 'Can we see the horses, Major?'

The officer gestured. 'Show him, Sergeant.' When he and the constable were alone, the officer looked steadily at Arch Trumbull when he spoke. 'By my lights, Constable, we got a bill of sale, the seller got his money an' as far as the army's concerned if there's trouble about who got paid an' who maybe wasn't Carlyle, that's the problem of civilians.'

Arch was expressionless and laconic when he replied, 'How about Stanton's branded horses?'

The major did not lower his gaze. 'He could have sold them to Carlyle, Constable.'

'There'd have to be a bill of sale, Major.'

The officer shook his head. 'That'd be between Carlyle an' Stanton, wouldn't it?'

Arch stood up. He hadn't expected such stubbornness. 'Did you take delivery?' he asked, and when the seated man nodded, the constable said, 'What did Carlyle look like, Major?'

'Shorter'n you, sort of dark like maybe part Mex or In'ian.'

Arch made a wintery smile. 'Ask your sergeant what Abraham Carlyle looked like: he helped us bury him.'

Will and the sergeant walked in and Stanton loudly said, 'My ten horses are with the others, Major. They was stole from me about a week back. I tracked 'em to that old man's corral.'

Major Maxwell was undisturbed by the rancher's agitation. He repeated what he had already said, 'We got a bill of sale for every horse brought here.'

Will Stanton reddened. 'Those branded animals belong to me. It's a registered brand an' I wouldn't have sold 'em, they were my best usin' animals.'

Arch Trumbull interrupted. 'This Mex-lookin' feller, did he say where he came from?'

The officer seemed relieved to be diverted from a

clearly angry cowman. 'Not to me,' he said. 'I gave him the army bill of sale form, he signed it, an' the quartermaster paid him in cash. Gentlemen, we badly needed those horses.'

Sergeant Fitzpatrick spoke, ignoring the annoyed officer's expression of disapproval. Fitzpatrick said, 'I went with him to his horse. He had three riders. They watched everything Carlyle, or whoever he was, did. As he was mounting, he told me he had more horses at his outfit north of Glorioso. He said any time we needed mounts to let him know an' he'd bring 'em. He told me the foothill country was full of 'em.'

Arch and the stockman exchanged a look as the major arose from his desk. He asked if the civilians wanted to see the bill of sale, and Arch shook his head as he started for the door.

Outside, Sergeant Fitzpatrick stood beside the constable's mount as he said, 'Maxwell goes by the book, an' to a point I got to agree with him. Findin' the feller who sold us the horses an' more'n likely killed that old man, ain't the army's business.' He stepped back as Arch evened his reins. 'Good luck,' he said.

Will Stanton would have hung back. He had found his stolen horses, but Arch Trumbull jerked his head for the stockman to follow him out of the compound with its tall palisade walls.

But Stanton's angry frustration had to have an outlet. He said, 'That miserable son of a bitch,' and launched into charges and recriminations most of which the constable had heard before.

It was late when they bypassed Glorioso and set a course for Cold Spring. For the most part the constable rode in silence, occupied with his thoughts, but when they left the road to settle for the night he said, 'I got a feelin' back there the only way you'll get back your horses is to find a fee lawyer.'

Stanton's response was to make a reckless statement. 'I'll get 'em back. That soldier's goin' to learn folks in this country don't go by any damned book.'

Fortunately it was a warm night and where they got into their bedrolls there was a creek and tall grass which would prevent their hobbled horses from going far.

Arch gazed upwards at millions of bright stars and got a feeling about those moccasins. Abraham Carlyle was an old man, well past the age when women would interest him and, by nature, he was a loner, one of those oldtimers whose view of a changing environment drove them to dislike almost everything about it.

Why, for instance, had the moccasins been hidden under blankets? For that matter, what impulse had driven him to rummage among the blankets?

He and Will Stanton were in the saddle while it was still dark. They had ridden quite a few miles before sunrise. They stopped twice to water and rest the horses, and for a change the husky cowman was mostly silent.

Cold Spring showed lights an hour or so before dusk but, by the time they reached the settlement, dusk had come and gone and darkness had arrived.

After their animals had been cared for they went to the eatery where the proprietor had been about to close up for the night, and was not pleased at having to stoke up the stove.

Afterwards they went over to the log jailhouse where the constable lighted a lamp and fired up the small iron stove. It was warm outside but not inside.

Stanton slumped in a chair. He said, 'The sergeant said the man who delivered the horses said there were more horses at his outfit up north. You expect he meant the old man's place?'

Arch had pondered that on the ride back. If he had known how many horses Carlyle had, it would have helped. He didn't know but suspected that the animals sold to the army would not be all the horses the old man either had caught or knew about in the foothill country.

He offered Stanton a place to bed down in his lean-to living-quarters but the cowman declined and left.

That was another worry for the constable. Stanton had said something about getting his horses back; all the constable needed was for the cowman to do something rash.

In the morning he was at the store when Jim Meeker walked in. He bought two sacks of tobacco and while rolling a brown-paper cigarette, his first of the day, he said, 'Them horses that was stampeded west of town some days back.' He paused to relight his quirley. 'There was three men drivin' 'em. Me'n Joe Parker rode out there. Joe can read sign better'n an In'ian.'

Arch nodded. He already knew there had been three riders.

'I'm not real good at readin' tracks but Joe pointed out somethin' to me that was interestin'. One of them shod horses had a toe cleat on a spreader shoe.'

Arch absorbed this scrap of information and later in the day when he met the saloonman at the eatery,

Joe confirmed what Meeker had told him. The saloonman also said, 'I got that old pelter Carlyle used in harness. I'm feedin' him up.'

At the look the constable put on Josiah Parker, the saloonman became defensive. 'Danged horse is older'n hell, part of his grinders are gone. He's been a hell of an animal in his day. It bothers me how folks treat 'em when they get old. Folks forget how many years they served 'em well. When they get old . . . I'm gettin' old too, Arch, maybe that's why I took in the old horse.'

4
Reasons to Ride

Arch left the settlement early. He made the trip alone despite a notion that it wasn't the smartest thing he had ever done.

When he emerged from tree-cover with the log house in sight his horse raised its head, little ears pointing. Arch came out of the gloom into sunlight and whether by instinct or exceptional hearing, the person crouching at the grave twisted, saw Arch coming and ran like a deer.

He went in pursuit. If the fleeing individual had gone north Arch couldn't have caught up, but the person ran west and that was meadow country for about half a mile.

There wasn't a human being alive who could outrun a horse. Arch came abreast, swung his horse hard and sent the runner sprawling. He dismounted and caught an ankle as the runner twisted to arise. Their eyes met from a distance of less than three feet. It was a woman!

Arch groped for a wrist and held it as he pulled the woman to her feet. She wasn't young, possibly in her late thirties or early forties. She had black

41

hair and eyes.

Arch said, 'If you try to run I'll tie you like a goat.'

The woman was expressionless. She was handsome without being pretty. She wore a doeskin skirt and a store-bought man's work shirt of faded blue.

He released her arm. 'Why did you run?' he asked.

She said nothing.

'I'm Arch Trumbull. I own the store in Cold Spring. I'm the constable too. What's your name?'

The woman gave look for look without opening her mouth.

Arch looked away long enough to make sure his horse wasn't wandering. It wasn't, but it was dragging the reins so Arch took the woman by the arm over to the horse where he hobbled the horse, removed the bridle and, while draping it from the saddlehorn he said, 'You don't have to talk, but when I get you back to the settlement an' lock you up, you'll talk or I'll throw the key away to the cage.'

The woman said, 'He was my father. I was putting a flat rock over his grave.'

'Abe Carlyle was your pa?'

'Yes.'

'Are you In'ian?'

'Yes. I live in the mountains. Why are you up here?'

Before answering Arch decided that whether the woman lived in the mountains or not, she spoke the kind of English people spoke who hadn't always lived apart.

He said, 'Sit down,' and after she sat he also eased down, and thumbed back his hat. 'What's your name?' he asked and this time she answered.

'Muriel Carlyle.'

Arch nodded. She was the M.C. beaded on to the moccasins he'd found. They regarded each other through a long moment of silence before he asked a question. 'Do you know who killed your father?' and her reply surprised him.

'I know. But I don't know why.'

'You saw it happen?'

'I was coming through the forest. Some men had been rounding up horses. I wanted to know why. He didn't sell horses. He trapped and gentled them. They were his family.'

'What did you see?'

'They were taking him from the house to the shed. He didn't walk right so they helped him.'

Arch nodded. They had helped him for a fact, from this world to the next one.

She spoke again. 'I had seen them. There were five of them. One was In'ian. Maybe Mexican. He was the boss. They worked many days rounding up horses. Two of them brought ten horses over the mountain; first I heard them then I went to a high place and watched them.'

'Where did they come from?' he asked.

She didn't know. 'They made camp in a place my father called miner's meadow. I saw their smoke but they had been there some days before I knew it. I don't know where they came from or where they went.'

'Have they come back?'

'Not to their camp. Maybe someplace else.'

'Where do you live?'

She raised an arm. 'Over there.' She lowered the arm. 'I lived with my mother. When she died I put her into the ground. I stayed. I had no other place to go. That was my home.'

'Not the old man's house?'

'No. When I was half grown my mother told him she wanted to go back and live the old way. He went with us and helped build a place for us. He came to see us but she wouldn't go back. I came to see my father many times. He taught me many things. He was kind.'

That didn't sound like the Abraham Carlyle Arch remembered, but he was willing to believe the old man loved his half-breed daughter.

She interrupted the flow of his reverie when she said, 'Where did they take the horses?'

'They sold them to the army.'

'But they couldn't do that, they were his horses.'

'Yes'm, they couldn't do it but they did. I want to find those men. If you know the mountains an' if they come back I could use some help.'

In the same easy way she had been speaking she said, 'I want to kill them.'

Arch shifted on the grass, made sure his horse was still close and finally looked at the handsome woman. She impressed him as being much younger than she was, not particularly in appearance but in the words she used and the way she spoke. She had clearly lost any fear she'd had of him. She even smiled at him. He decided she was a product of isolation, she had trust and candour. He plucked a blade of grass and chewed it. She studied him and said, 'My mother told me that someday a man would come.'

Arch got rid of the grass stalk. 'Is there a way you can let me know when those men come back?'

She was doubtful. 'I can't make a signal fire. They will see it. I am afraid of them, but the mountains are wide and deep, they'll never catch me if I know they will try.'

Arch made a little lopsided grin. 'I caught you,' he said.

Her answer was naïve. 'Because you had a horse.'

He nodded. The horsethieves would also have horses. 'Wasn't it hard going back and forth between your parents?'

'No. Do you love someone?' Before he could answer she also said, 'I loved them both. I tried for years to get my mother to move back to the log house. She said old people are most comfortable living the old way.'

He glanced at the position of the sun, arose and dusted himself off and held out a hand. She looked briefly bewildered then took it and allowed him to bring her up to her feet. She withdrew the hand and considered his horse. 'Good animal,' she told Arch. 'Good bone, good muscle. My father loved horses.'

It was time to head back; he told her he wanted to see her again. She said, 'When you come I'll know,' and watched him ride back the way he had come.

Again it was dark when he reached the settlement but this time the caféman still had a light showing, which was good because the constable was hungry enough to eat a bear if someone would hold its head.

In the morning he returned to the eatery and was fed again. Afterwards he went looking for Will Stanton. The horse-trading blacksmith said he had seen the cowman leave the settlement early, riding south.

When he opened the store, Mary Elkins came up behind him and said, 'Well, it's about time you minded the business.'

He could have agreed, instead he told the older woman he might have to leave Cold Spring for a day or two and her retort was typically acerbic. 'Why shouldn't you? You're never here anyway. I suppose you'll want me to mind the place while you're gone.' When the constable nodded, the dowdy, greying woman made a sniffing sound. 'I know the symptoms. You're chasin' after a woman. Well, good luck to you. I'll mind the store until you get back.'

He rode south and continued riding after nightfall. He wasn't hopeful of overtaking Stanton but he felt obliged to make the attempt.

He had plenty to think about so time passed quickly. It was still dark but with the usual predawn chill increasing when he saw the tiny fire a mile or so easterly and left the road riding toward it.

The cowman did not act surprised when the constable reined up. 'By Gawd I got a right,' he said defensively. 'Bill of sale or no bill of sale they got my horses.'

Arch swung down. 'How you figure to get 'em? They're corralled inside the compound. There'll be sentries guardin' the gate.' Arch squatted. 'I told you once before, there's no ten saddle animals in the world worth gettin' killed over.'

Stanton shook a small skillet. 'You had supper?'

'Breakfast,' the constable said. 'I had supper last night. Listen to me, Mister Stanton, if the army's got a bill of sale, forged or not, that's all they'll need. Like the major said, they took delivery an' paid cash. As far as the army's concerned they own the horses.'

'Not my animals they don't.'

'Your animals too. You heard him; he done what he was supposed to do, beyond that it's a civilian matter.'

'An' what civilian law is there in this country?'

Arch stood up trailing the reins to his hip-shot, dozing horse. 'Ride back with me an' I'll tell you what I figure Cold Spring law can do.'

'No!'

Arch regarded the stockman through a moment of silence, then spoke again. 'You got a woman an' kids. If they get you back in a pine box nothing's ever goin' to convince them you were worth ten damned horses. Now saddle up an' ride back with me.'

Stanton considered his tiny fire, arose and smothered it with scuffed soil. He rigged out his mount, stowed the little fry pan, stepped up across leather and said, 'You got an idea?'

Arch nodded from the saddle, turned and led off in the direction of the road. While riding through a moonless night he told Stanton about his visit to the Carlyle place and finding the 'breed woman there. He told the stockman what she had said and concluded by saying, 'If you think on it, you'll get to the notion that whoever them horsethieves are, they're a country mile from being greenhorns at the stealin' business.'

Stanton said, 'Five? I thought there was two, maybe three.' The constable dogged it at a walk for nearly a mile before Stanton spoke by asking again, 'You got an idea?'

Arch had. 'We go up there tomorrow night when they won't be able to see riders. Take some riders with us. As many as we can get. The woman knows them mountains up'n down an' sideways. She knows where they had a camp. We may not need her if we reach the uplands before dawn. They'll likely have a breakfast fire goin'.'

Will Stanton looped both reins, lifted his hat and vigorously scratched. When he unlooped the reins he said, 'How many posse riders?'

Arch had no idea. Cold Spring was a settlement, neither a village nor a town, and if folks knew why he needed armed riders they could be expected to avoid being conscripted.

Stanton could have read the constable's mind because he said, 'How about rangemen? We could make a gather on the way up there.'

Arch's mood brightened. 'Good idea,' he exclaimed and said no more until they had the settlement in sight. As they were dismounting, the stockman had another suggestion to make but it was prompted more by enthusiasm than common sense. 'You could send a rider to the fort, get the army to come up here.'

Arch put a rueful look on his companion without saying a word. Stanton took the silent rebuke without trying to defend the idea. He wanted to know when they would ride and the constable said, 'Tomorrow night. I'll see if I can get riders close by. Otherwise we'll start earlier tomorrow night so's we can sashay among the ranches.'

The following morning Jim Meeker had a hay fork poised when someone groaned in his haystack. He leaned on the fork as Will Stanton emerged, stood up brushing off hay. The blacksmith made a common remark to someone arising from spending the night bedded in a stack of hay.

'Fifty feet from the stack to pee.'

Stanton rubbed both eyes, considered the other man and nodded. Meeker forked feed into his corral and left the fork sticking in the stack as he dryly said, 'Mister, I never charged for burrowin' into my hay, but if you figure to do this often it's goin' to cost you two bits a night.'

Stanton was still picking hay off when he arrived at the eatery. It was evidently too early, or too late, for the caféman's regulars so he had the counter to himself.

He had almost finished breakfast when Josiah Parker, the saloonman, walked in. He nodded, sat down, ordered, then gazed at the only other diner. 'You 'n the constable been riding together a lot lately,' he said and, as Stanton nodded, the saloon-man also said, 'You missed him this mornin'. I saw him ridin' westerly before daylight.'

Stanton nodded again, arose, spilled coins beside his empty platter and left the eatery.

He had to guess why the constable had left so early, but a man couldn't associate with another man for any length of time to pretty well anticipate him; he was satisfied the constable had changed his mind about wasting time rousting out rangemen, he'd gone to do that early so that when the posse was ready it would be in full force.

The saloonman emerged from the eatery sucking his teeth, saw the stockman leaning against an over-hang upright and said, 'Hard feller to get to know.'

Stanton nodded without looking at the other man.

'I'll tell you one thing, a man that's got a business can't make ends meet ridin' all over hell,' Parker exclaimed.

Stanton faced around. 'Get yourself another constable then, so Trumbull can mind his store.'

Joe Parker hadn't liked the waspish way his

comment had been answered and turned northward. By the time he had entered the saloon he missed seeing Tim Farrel enter town from the west.

Stanton watched the cowman also go north. He tied up to an old stud ring embedded in a huge cottonwood tree in front of a small cottage. Farrel knocked several times before giving up, retracing his steps, but instead of mounting, he led his horse southward as far as the general store where he again tied the animal, this time to a hitch rack, and disappeared inside.

Moments later what sounded like a cat screeching on a hot tin roof made Stanton turn. It was a female in the store making that racket. Occasionally but not often a man's voice sounded, but more soothing than angry.

An old woman carrying a mesh shopping bag came abreast of Will Stanton, cocked her head and said, 'Like a pair of cougar cubs in a croaker sack,' and went on her way.

She disappeared in the store and the argument ended as Farrel emerged from the store looking left and right. He saw Stanton and the fact that they were strangers to one another made less difference than the fact that they were males.

Farrel walked up and said, 'There's nothin' on this earth as contrary as women!'

Will nodded because obviously this was what was expected. The rancher wasn't finished. 'It ain't that she'd do better'n place last in a beauty contest an' barely scrapes by what with her sewin' an' mindin' the store.'

Farrel checked himself up, regarded Stanton and shoved out a calloused hand. 'Tim Farrel, I run cattle north-west of here.'

Will pumped the older man's hand as he said, 'Will Stanton. I got cattle an' horses on the far side of the mountains in a place called Hideout Valley.'

Having established a mutual interest Farrel said, 'Stand you to a drink, Mister Stanton,' and on their way northward he also said, 'Aren't you the feller folks says been ridin' out with the constable lately?'

Stanton answered while holding aside one spindle door for the older man to enter the saloon first. 'We been ridin' together, for a fact. Someone stole ten of my horses an' I tracked 'em to the corral of an old feller named Carlyle.'

Joe Parker put up two glasses and a bottle and was about to walk away when Farrel said, 'Abe Carlyle's corral? Mister, I've known Abe since you was in short pants. He'd never steal horses.'

'I didn't say he stole them; I said they were in his corral. He's dead.'

Farrel's glass was almost to his mouth when it stopped moving. 'Abe Carlyle's dead?'

'Got beat to death with an axe handle.'

'When?'

'Some time back.'

Joe Parker put in his two bits worth. 'From what I know about old Carlyle it'd take an almighty coyote individual to get close carryin' a club.'

Stanton ignored the saloonman. 'That's mostly why me'n the constable been ridin' out. Right now I'm waitin' for him to come back from tryin' to raise posse riders.'

Farrel put the glass down untouched. 'Posse riders for what?'

'It's a long story,' Stanton said. 'You want to hear it

we'd better go to a table.' As they left the bar Joe Parker's frustrated curiosity drove him to polishing his back-bar row of bottles with a feather duster. He did this with unaccustomed vigour.

By the time Will Stanton had finished his recitation Timothy Farrel was stunned into silence, but eventually he said, 'Frank Maxwell's my cousin. I don't like him, avoid bein' anywhere he's at, but I can tell you one thing about him, he's honest an' fair.'

Will's reply was dry. 'He didn't leave me feelin' he was like that.'

'He's a career soldier, Mister Stanton, they don't think like we do. I ain't been to see him since he turned up as commander down at Fort Buchanan.' Farrel downed a jolt, blew out a flammable breath and changed the subject. 'Arch is out tryin' to round up posse riders? Well now, I got four riders, two full-time, two seasonal. I'll have 'em in Cold Spring before sundown.'

Will Stanton smiled. 'That'll be a starter, Mister Farrel. Me'n the constable will be real obliged.'

The rancher stood up. 'Abe Carlyle an' me was friends. Been friends about twenty years. He wasn't a real easy man to like but we shared notions ... I didn't know the old goat had a daughter.'

Will also arose. 'Neither did the constable.'

5

Toward a New Day

Arch Trumbull didn't return to the settlement until the sun was low. He had three rangemen with him. He introduced them to Will Stanton and the five of them went to the eatery where the proprietor was busier than a kitten in a box of shavings. He took orders, nodded, and padded to his kitchen. One of the recruited rangemen, a dark man named Bert Fellows, was interested in what Will Stanton had to say about his ten horses. When Will finished the dark man said, 'I never met Carlyle but from what I've heard he was as honest as the day is long.'

As they were leaving the café, five men appeared in the doorway. Tim Farrel introduced his riders, said they'd eaten at the ranch and were ready to ride. One of Farrel's hired hands was tall, very tall, and correspondingly thin. He had a prominent Adam's apple. His name was Norman Abbot. He was called Jack and despite his ungainly appearance Tim Farrel leaned close to tell the constable that Jack Abbot was the best shot with a handgun the cowman had ever met.

The constable waited until they were all outside

before he explained what he knew, what he suspected and what he intended to do. Any time the word 'horsethief' was mentioned, rangemen just naturally bristled. Murdering horsethieves could be guaranteed to make rangemen who had no interest in risking their lives, willing volunteers.

It was while the men were out front of the eatery that Josiah Parker and the horse-trading blacksmith, Jim Meeker, came along wearing sidearms and carrying carbines. The constable willingly accepted their volunteering to ride along and left the men to introduce themselves. Mostly, the settlement men were known among the rangemen. Jim Meeker offered horses to those who were afoot and got no takers. Everyone had mounts. Meeker made a sly comment to Will Stanton. 'You won't burrow into my haystack tonight,' and Stanton smiled.

People appeared on both sides of the road to watch. They weren't clear about the purpose nor the reason for heavily armed men to be in front of the café, but they'd heard enough to be both curious and interested. When the riders broke up, some to get horses, the others to lean on hitch racks where their animals were tethered, one man, the tousle-headed parson, crossed over and accosted Tim Farrel. The cowman was brusque and evasive.

Dusk was close when the possemen left the settlement by way of the northerly stage road. After they were gone the speculative gossip mill started. Someone even suggested the constable was leading his companions against Indians, and there hadn't been an Indian in the Cold Spring country for about a generation.

It was a warm evening and there was even a new

moon. It gave no appreciable light but there were enough stars to augment it, so visibility was fair.

Mostly, the riders knew the country, although precious few had dared go toward Abraham Carlyle's land. Even after Arch led them up the old rutted road toward the log house, while there was no comment, it was noticeable that the men sat straighter in their saddles.

Tim Farrel reminisced. He'd done an occasional favour for Carlyle, such as fetching back the old man's strayed horses and once, when Abraham was abed with the grippe, Farrel had brought medicine from the settlement and had sat with Carlyle until he was able to get around.

He said they had talked, but it was a time before the old man opened up, just a little, and he'd never mentioned women. He'd talked about Indian scrapes, exploring and scouting, and his horses, which Farrel said left the cowman wondering if the old man's fondness for horses wasn't the result of Abraham having no family and few friends.

He concluded his recitation by saying, 'I heard years back he had a woman, but so help me Hannah, it surprised the hell out of me to hear he had a daughter.'

The constable abruptly drew rein. He had seen nothing, neither had the others. They were quiet.

Like a ghost the woman appeared in the roadway ahead. She stood like a statue until Arch spoke. 'Muriel . . . where are they?'

'I'm not sure. They struck their old camp. But they're up here; I saw smoke and went following the smell.' She raised an arm. 'Ride that way, you'll smell smoke.'

She disappeared on the north side of the road where huge, overripe pines and firs stood in solid ranks.

Jim Meeker had a question. 'Is that Carlyle's daughter?'

No one answered as Arch rode a few yards ahead before leaving the road. He paused in a clearing, suggested they spread out and whoever saw a fire or smelled smoke was to alert the others.

Will Stanton rode with the constable. 'If I was in their boots,' he said, 'I'd never come back to this country.'

'You might,' the constable retorted, 'if there was more horses to be gathered, an' if you didn't know we was after you.'

The cowman had nothing more to say as he and the constable dodged back and forth through timber riding northerly. It was darker in the timbered highlands than it was back yonder in open country, and there were sounds men would rarely hear elsewhere. Bears, who preferred to forage by daylight grumbled and bumped a lot, and although both wolves and coyotes were silent, the occasional scream of a cougar didn't bother the men as much as it frightened their horses.

What the constable probably should have anticipated, happened. The unearthly stillness was shattered by a single gunshot which, after an interval, was followed by a second gunshot.

Arch and the cowman placed the direction from the second shot and altered their direction accordingly. Others who had also heard the gunshots also sashayed among the huge trees in almost total darkness, riding by instinct.

Caution was the uppermost concern, and being cautious took time. There were no more gunshots but there was something else, the sound of running horses. It was impossible to determine the course the horses were taking because it sounded as though individual horses went in different directions.

They found a horse whose reins had got tangled in undergrowth. It was standing with the patience of a tethered animal, but raised its head as the sound of approaching riders seemed to come from several directions.

When Arch and Will got close, the riderless horse fidgeted but its reins remained fast. It could not escape.

A man with the voice of a fighting bull roared curses, he was not immediately visible but the direction of his voice led the possemen to him. It was Joe Parker, the saloonman. He was sitting on the ground, his back to a tree holding his left arm. The possemen had to dismount and get close before they saw the blood. Parker said, 'I didn't see the son of a bitch until I damned near rode over him. It seemed to surprise him as much as it did me, but he shot first an' I fell off the horse. I got off one shot but it's so damned dark up here . . . lend me a hand.'

They got the saloonman upright leaning against his tree. Meeker the blacksmith tore the bloody sleeve, wrapped it tightly around the bullet wound in Parker's upper arm, and twisted it until the bleeding stopped.

Parker looked apologetically at the constable. 'I was watchin' real close,' he said, and Arch's response was quietly offered. 'It could have been any one of us, Joe.'

Tim Farrel and his long-shanked rider rode through the trees, guns in hand. The first thing they found was a small clearing where burnt-out stumps showed that the clearing had been the result of a lightning strike. The second thing they found was where horses had been hobbled to graze.

Horse sign indicated that the animals had been on the clearing for some time, possibly three or four days.

Eventually the men congregated around the saloonman who profanely insisted that he could ride. Among his growling statements was that if he caught the man who had shot him, when he was finished the man's own mother wouldn't recognize him.

Arch favoured sending the saloonman back to the settlement with an escort. To this Joe Parker protested so fiercely that the subject was dropped.

When Farrel and his rider returned to say what they had found, someone swore and said that now they wouldn't be able to find the horsethieves, and worse, the horsethieves now knew they were being hunted. This unhappy individual suggested they turn back, that maybe come daylight they could pick up some tracks.

After a long silence Arch wondered if they shouldn't continue the hunt. No one seemed to think this was a good idea so the constable said, 'You fellers go back,' and the tall Farrel rider said, 'An' you?'

'Sashay around; come dawn there should be tracks. I want one of them. All of them for a fact, but right now I'll settle for one.'

If there were dissenters they remained silent. As the riders fanned out in a south-westerly direction, which it had sounded as though several of the fleeing renegades had gone, they progressed with more caution than before. Joe Parker had his injured arm tucked inside his shirt. It was swelling, which made the impromptu bandage tighter, and the pain had been steadily increasing after the shooting.

Parker, the saloonman, had a remedy of sorts: a bottle of brandy in his saddle-bag on the right side. He was able to fumble the buckle loose, and drank deeply. Afterwards he offered the bottle around, got no takers and stowed it back where it had come from as he made panting sounds during which he profanely said that brandy burned going down and burned when it got settled.

It was one of those rare summer nights when the cold came surreptitiously. The riders had covered a considerable distance in width but not much otherwise. There were remarks about riding blind. There were also comments about riding into an ambush, but with the advent of first light in open country, almost no brightness got past the splayed tops of ancient trees, nor was there much warmth until they unexpectedly left the gloom and timber to draw rein on the east edge of a farmed clearing.

The log house had smoke rising from a stone fireplace. There were two mules and a horse in a large corral, and a goat who saw the party of horsemen moving across the farmed clearing and stood stonestill until it bleated and went to the cabin's door. A rider laughed. 'I know about watch dogs,' he said, 'but that's the first watch goat I ever saw.'

A youngish man appeared in the doorway watching as the possemen rode toward the house. The goat moved warily away. Its bleat of alarm had alerted the mules and the horse. They lined up along the corral also watching.

Arch raised his right hand, palm forward, the ancient sign of friendship. The man reached inside. When he faced forward he had a double-barrelled shotgun in his hands.

Arch stopped about twenty feet from the man, introduced himself, explained who his companions were and the settler leaned aside his scattergun and gestured. 'Three fellers went past last night. The goat got me out of bed, but by the time I come out there was only echoes.' The settler considered the men with the constable before also saying, 'They went due west. About three miles from here there's two other homesteaders. Maybe they seen 'em.' Again the settler paused before speaking. 'Them horses look like they could do with a bait of hay an' some barley, an' you gents might be hungry. I'm not a good cook but you're sure welcome.'

Arch expressed his gratitude for the offer but told the settler he didn't want to lose time. For this last remark he got several looks of exasperation from his companions.

They continued on around the log house and, where sunlight touched, Tim Farrel picked up tracks. They followed them at a lope until they encountered timber again, thereafter they made slower progress.

The sun was climbing when Will Stanton said he smelled wood smoke. He was right but they had to skirt some post and rider fences before they reached the pair of houses and, as before, they didn't surprise anyone, but this time it was a brace of long-haired large brown dogs that brought a man outside.

Again the constable explained who he was and why he and his companions were in the uplands. The homesteader, big enough to eat hay with a full beard, offered feed for the possemen and their horses. Arch might not have accepted if the giant hadn't come closer and spoke in a lowered voice. 'We maybe got one of them fellers you're after. His horse missed jumpin' a deadfall. The feller's inside laid up from the fall. His horse run off.'

The bearded man had barely stopped speaking when a wiry, rumpled dark man came from out of the house with a cocked gun in his fist.

He didn't address the constable, he spoke to the big bearded man. 'I told you, anyone came by an' you said anythin' I'd blow your wife's head off.'

The man was crouched. He was also without his boots. No one moved nor spoke. The dark man eased up slightly. 'Get off them horses,' he exclaimed. Arch and his companions saw a very large woman glide soundlessly from the doorway. They leaned to dismount, which held the dark man's attention. The woman struck him over the head with an iron skillet. His gun went off as he fell.

The big bearded man walked over and put his foot on the unconscious man's back and glared at his wife. 'You could have got killed,' he said, and the large woman answered curtly, 'He'd have shot you. I was behind him. Well, carry him inside, don't just stand there.' The horsemen dismounted, several were grinning.

Tim Farrel said, 'If she wasn't so big . . .' and did not complete the sentence as he watched the bearded man lift the limp dark man as though he were a child and march toward the house.

The woman told them to corral their horses. She said there was fresh timothy in the barn and, as she was facing toward the house she also said, "There's lye soap in a can by the trough. I'll make up something to eat.'

There was no doubt about who ran this homestead. Farrel's tall rider forked feed and afterward leaned on the fork to say, 'Now there's a female woman a man could cotton to.'

They washed, trooped into the house and Arch was surprised at its size until Jim Meeker said, 'Big folks make things to scale.'

The woman took Joe Parker to her kitchen. The men could hear him groaning as the bearded man introduced himself. 'I'm Heber Finch. That's my wife. Her name is Angel Finch.'

No one showed expression. Angel Finch was the biggest, stoutest, hard-headedest angel they had ever imagined.

Angel Finch's iron skillet was heavy enough to crack boulders. The dark, wiry man she had struck did not come around until the possemen had finished eating. He said his name was Walter Jones and that he'd been riding alone when his horse tried to jump a deadfall tree and didn't clear it. He had the grandaddy of all headaches.

Angel Finch brought him half a glass of elderberry wine which he downed in three swallows and held up the glass, but the large woman shook her head. 'It's for medicine, Mister Jones, not for drinking otherwise,' and left the small room where the dark man sat on the edge of a handmade bed.

He would have arisen but the bearded man put a hand the size of a ham on his chest and held him in place as he said, 'Your ankle won't heal if you push things. Where did you get that pistol?'

'Out of the holster in your bedroom,' the dark man replied, looking up. 'I'd have. . . .'

'You'd have got yourself killed,' the large man said quietly. 'You shot off the only round in my pistol.'

Angel Finch shouldered her way past the posse-men and told her husband the injured man in the kitchen needed someone to go out to his saddle and fetch a bottle in the offside saddle-bag.

The big man and his wife exchanged a long, solemn look before she said, 'It'll have to be all right, but you'd ought to take him outside. You know what the covenant says.'

Her husband solemnly nodded and left the room. The woman leaned to consider the lump on the head of the dark man and made a clucking sound. 'I didn't mean to hit you so hard you'd get a lump big as a goose egg.'

Jones looked up. 'That fry pan is solid iron, lady.'

She pushed past on her way back to the kitchen where the saloonman had one-handedly helped himself to a few swallows of elderberry wine and was waiting when she entered eyeing him sceptically. 'What'd Mister Jones do that got half an army after him?'

'Stole horses, killed an old man, sold the horses to the army on a forged bill of sale an' come back to steal more horses.'

'Where are the others?'

'Hell, lady, I got no idea, but we'll track 'em.'

'And if you catch them, Mister Parker?'

'Hang 'em, ma'am.'

'The Lord says he will punish transgressors. It's in the Bible.'

Joe Parker was feeling less pain by the minute.

'Ma'am, I'm crowdin' sixty. I can tell you the Lord ain't interested in what folks on earth do or he'd have prevented the Civil War. Is your husband a preacher?'

She gave the saloon man look for look when she replied. 'He's a bishop. We're saintly folk. Brigham Young's our patron. How does the arm feel?'

The saloonman was still digesting what she had said so his reply about the injured arm was slow coming. 'Laudanum'd help, ma'am. I don't expect you'd have any?'

'We don't,' she retorted and leaned to examine her job of cleaning and bandaging the arm. She didn't commiserate beyond straightening up as she said, 'Jehovah favoured you, Mister Parker. It's a flesh wound, no broke bones. You got to keep it clean otherwise you'll get blood poisoning.'

She went to the huge cook stove, fed wood into the fire box and when she heard her husband return from the barn she told Joe Parker to go outside with her husband, which Joe did without any idea why she wanted him out of her house.

The huge bearded man handed Joe the bottle of brandy, watched him take down two healthy jolts and when the saloonman held out the bottle the bearded man considered it, shot a quick look in the direction of the house, grasped the bottle and also swallowed twice, handed back the bottle, wiped watering eyes and breathed loudly through his mouth as he told Parker not to tell his wife and Joe agreed as he put the bottle inside his shirt.

The bearded man breathed in noisy gusts. He asked what was in the bottle, and when Parker said it was brandy, the big man rolled his eyes. 'Lord

preserve me from ever tastin' brandy again. It burns.'
He coughed and rolled his eyes. 'That's my punishment, Mister Parker.'

Angel appeared in the doorway. She had a meal
prepared. She looked long and hard at her husband
as the bearded man and Joe Parker started toward
the door.

6
Horsebacking

The horses badly needed feed and rest. Arch went out to the corral with Will Stanton who anticipated the constable when he said, 'We got to spend the night here.'

Arch nodded agreement. He'd briefly thought about commandeering the pair of mules and the saddle animal but Will Stanton said, 'Them's harness mules. Did you ever try to ride a mule that's not broke to saddle?'

Arch hadn't. He sighed and considered the sky. There wasn't a cloud in sight, just millions of stars and that scimitar moon.

The saloonman went to sit with the man calling himself Walter Jones, the other posse riders joined Stanton and the constable at the corral. The cowman, Farrel, said, 'A fresh start in the mornin' ought to help, specially if those bastards gun-runnin' an' bedded down. As hard as they used their horses they'd better take time off.'

Homesteaders with no use for bunkhouses did not have them, and the separate log house a dozen or so yards from the Finch house turned out to offer little encouragement. It had no floor, no windows and a door that stood closed but hadn't been hinged yet.

Angel left it to her husband to find places for the posse riders to bed down. He was apologetic but promised them a hearty breakfast come daylight. He explained about the unfinished house; he'd been building it for about a year in his spare time. He and his wife had a married daughter, her parents had decided to build the house and give it to her for a Christmas present, sort of an inducement for the daughter and her husband to come and live close by.

Angel wanted to keep Joe Parker in the house, which might have been agreeable to the saloonman but there was only one spare bedroom and the wiry, dark horsethief was occupying it.

Joe tried to tastefully explain to the large woman that since his arm no longer hurt, he'd prefer bedding down with the constable and the others.

Angel did not protest but after the saloonman had left and her husband returned, she told him she wasn't really unhappy because Mister Parker owned a saloon, and someone like that staying overnight in their house might very well incite a calamitous heavenly retribution.

Stanton, the constable, Tim Farrel and Joe Parker unrolled their blankets on the lee side of a varmint-proof hen house whose inhabitants had gone to roost after sunset and would not be noisy until sunrise.

As the saloonman eased down he said, 'That scrawny 'breed or whatever he is, is named Antonio Flores.' His companions waited until Joe got settled favouring the arm inside his shirt. He also said, 'The head In'ian of them horsethieves is a 'breed named

Earl Hampshire, an' he goes by the name of Pancho Jefferson. Arch, you figured it about right.'

Farrel had a question. 'He told you all this?'

'I told him I'd brain him if he lied and held my six-gun ready to do it. He started talkin' like a damned parrot.

'This Pancho Jefferson bastard an' another feller scouted up the Carlyle place for a couple of weeks, then went over the mountains and stole them Stanton horses which they'd planned to do before they found the old man's place with all the horses.

'They went back, stole the Stanton horses an' drove 'em over the mountains to the Carlyle place, left 'em with some other horses, went down and killed the old man. They then put the branded horses in the old man's corral and went to make a gather. You know the rest, they drove 'em to the fort an' sold 'em.' Again the saloonman paused. 'This Pancho feller come back to make another gather of the old man's horses, an' had it all figured when we come on to 'em.'

After the saloonman was quiet his listeners lay back in silence until sleep arrived. In the morning they cleaned up at the trough and trooped to the house where Angel had been busy since before sunrise. Her husband was out back fetching stove wood when the possemen entered. He dumped his armload and called a booming 'Good morning', and before they could answer he also said, 'He got away in the night.'

No one moved. Arch said, 'That scrawny horsethief?' and the large man nodded. He also said, 'He's got a cracked ankle an' a hurt back. You hadn't ought to have much trouble runnin' him down.'

Tim Farrel said, 'He didn't steal your horse?'

'He wouldn't want to do that,' the big man stated. 'Nobody's ever rode that horse. He works good in drivin' harness but he can't be rode. How about your horses?'

Farrel's stringbean with the prominent Adam's apple answered. 'They was all there when I forked feed,' and shook his head. 'Good thing he didn't try, I been sleepin' with one eye open for years.'

Angel brusquely called, 'It's on the table. While you're eating I'll make up a bundle.' The large homesteader had his own style of eating. As with many men with full beards he raised food directly in front of his face and from a distance of about four inches opened his mouth and put the forkful into its place without touching a hair.

The sun was fully above the easterly horizon when the posse riders got rigged out ready to ride. Arch thanked Angel and her husband. Tim Farrel did something more substantial; he rode beside the porch where Angel was standing and held out his hand. When she reached Farrel dropped two silver cartwheels on to her palm, reined around and joined the other riders on their westerly way out of the yard.

Farrel had to quarter to pick up the trail, which was clear enough to a watchful tracker, but less clear than it would have been if that rat-eyed skinny person calling himself Jones hadn't lost his horse.

Jim Meeker and one or two others groused about someone's lack of concern about either chaining the wiry dark man or standing watch over him last night, until Josiah Parker said, 'Short of hangin' the scrawny bastard, which I don't think Angel would have stood for if we used her barn baulk, what could we do with him? He was hurt an' afoot an' he didn't say anythin' more'n we needed. Far as I'm concerned he can wander these mountains until a cougar eats him.'

They watered the animals at a willow-lined creek and continued tracking. Tim Farrel's ability to read sign impressed the others. Jim Meeker eventually said something complimentary and the cowman replied without looking up.

'When you've tracked as many hideout mammy cows and sore-footed bulls as I have you learn a little, and these lads got horses diggin' in with their hind feet, makin' sign a baby could read.'

The sun was directly overhead by the time the possemen breasted a long landswell with excellent visibility in all directions.

Except for an occasional small party of wet cows with their calves the land was empty. Stanton sat with Tim Farrel as the latter said, 'Well, if they crossed this country they must've had wings.'

Behind the pair of ranchers, Bert Fellows, by nature a taciturn man, said, 'Foller the tracks, sure as hell they changed course because they aren't out ahead nowhere.'

That is what Tim Farrel did, but where the tracks bent around southward, while this too was open grassland, they saw no riders, Although Farrel boosted his animal over into a lope, paralleling the tracks, they were unable to catch sight of riders and they held to a lope for better than a mile.

Farrel hauled back down to a steady walk as he wagged his head in disgust. He didn't say a word. He didn't have to, every posse rider was just as disgusted.

Joe Parker used one of their stops to take 'medicine'. He didn't offer the bottle around; it was close to being empty.

They had an unusual encounter in cow country. First, they saw the shepherd's wagon, one of those rigs with a rounded canvas top, next they saw the dogs, three of them standing like statues watching the approaching posse riders. They didn't bark until a lean, dark man wearing ill-fitting, faded and patched workclothes appeared. The last thing they saw was sheep, about a hundred of them. They either did not see riders or weren't interested. They were grazing and browsing.

Neither the constable nor his companions said a word, they were too shocked.

When they reached the wagon the thin shepherd smiled and offered coffee which no one accepted as they sat their saddles. Jim Meeker spoke first. 'These your woollies?'

The dark man stopped smiling as he answered. 'Yes. I had more but someone shot them.' He decided the man wearing the badge was the leader of the strangers and addressed him. 'My name is Henry Arro. I am grazing southward. I came from Wyoming where they kill sheep.' Henry Arro paused. He was facing a band of silent, unsmiling men. He was probably frightened but did not show it. 'In the southern country I was told there are sheep an' down there they don't shoot sheepmen.'

He was partly right, Mexicans on both sides of the border ran sheep – and goats. Except for the extreme heat of summer sheep fared better than cattle or horses; sheep would eat any kind of brush. As for shooting shepherds, that was no more common down yonder than it was most other places where sheepmen ran their animals.

Arch asked if Henry Arro had seen riders and the thin, dark man raised his arm. 'Two on rode-down horses. They watered at my trough. I gave them some wine and they left. Are they Indians?'

Arch ignored the question. 'How long ago an' which way did they go?'

'It was before daylight an' when they left they went south. I watched; they kept going south.'

Josiah Parker made no attempt to stifle the groan. As they left the shepherd he said, 'Messico sure as hell, an' with a good lead they'll get down there before we find 'em.'

Arch slouched along for a while then straightened in the saddle. 'No sense in keepin' this up,' he told his companions and reined easterly in the direction of Cold Spring. They arrived there in late afternoon riding tucked-up horses. When Arch finished at the eatery and went to the store Mary Elkins was waiting. 'Done eleven dollars worth of trade today. That's pretty good. How much good did you do?'

The constable got a cigar from a case, lighted it and eyed the dowdy, sharp-tongued woman. 'We did some good. Why; folks interested, are they?'

'What would you expect? In this settlement even a dog fight keeps folks talkin' until something else comes along. By the way, is that feller from over the mountain married?'

'Will Stanton? He's married with kids.' Arch tipped ash before speaking again. 'Why don't you cotton with Tim Farrel, he's fixed for life, is even tempered, don't drink much?'

The older woman blushed. 'Once was enough,' she replied, and changed the subject. 'You know that

fuzzy-faced freighter that talks like he's got a mouthful of hot potatoes?'

Everyone knew Curtis Middleton, he was the only
freighter who consistently brought supplies to the
settlement. 'Curt Middleton? I know him. Why?'

'Well, he found a crippled-up, starvin' runt of a
Mex on the road up near Frenchman's Gulch. Feller
could hardly walk. He told fuzzy-face, whatever his
name is, that his horse bucked him off. He hurt his
leg an' his back, an' he'd been hobblin' all night and
most of this mornin' to find the road.'

The cigar was cold so Arch removed it. 'Where is
he? Not the freighter, the man he found?'

'Up at the parson's place . . . where are you goin'?'

At the door Arch said, 'I'll be back directly,' and
crossed the road on his way toward the northernmost
end of the settlement.

The minister was a tousle-headed individual, one
of the rare ones who didn't wear his collar backwards. When Arch met him, the minister said, 'I had
a guest; short, stringy man with close-set eyes like a
weasel. Curt Middleton found him alongside the
road and dropped him off out front. He's got an
ankle swore as big as a melon an' a bad back.'

Arch scowled. 'You *had* him?'

'When I was in the study working on Sunday's
sermon he stole my horse'n saddle. I don't know
which way he went but I'd guess from his colouring
he went south.'

As the constable was on his way back to the store,
Josiah Parker hailed him from across the road to say
the midwife wasn't at her house. Arch told him she
was at the store and the saloonman called back he
needed his arm looked at.

Will Stanton was leaving the store when the constable entered and told the cowman what he'd learned from the parson. Stanton allowed Arch to get it all said before speaking.

'There's a right handsome In'ian woman waitin' at the jailhouse. She told me she's the daughter of old Carlyle, an' I'll tell you one thing, she's as nervous as a caged 'coon.'

Arch crossed to the log structure and when he walked in Muriel Carlyle leapt out of the chair she'd been sitting in.

Arch smiled, tossed his hat aside and gestured for her to sit back down. She remained standing. Arch said, 'It's a long walk. Couldn't you have found a horse?'

She stood very erect, her dark eyes were wide open. She spoke as though she hadn't heard the constable.

'They're back. Not all of them, only four. They're at the old camp. Their horses are in bad shape.'

Arch stared. 'You're sure they're back. Because we tracked two of 'em almost as far south as Glorioso.'

She was adamant. 'I heard them and went through the forest to watch them arrive and turn their horses loose. I wasn't close enough to hear but they talked much. The one I think is their leader is named Pancho. He was walking away when one man called to him. I think he called him Pancho.'

That clinched it for the constable, she had heard the right name, but why and how they had ridden all the way back to the uplands baffled him, until she eventually said, 'Do you know where my father's horse trap is?'

Arch shook his head. The woman was briefly silent

before saying, 'Before they made the other camp, closer to the trap, they rounded up many horses. They didn't get them into the trap. Wild horses are smart.'

Arch interrupted. 'Where is the horse trap?'

'Do you know where their second camp was?'

Arch knew and nodded. He would never forget that place.

'The horse trap is a deep arroyo where my father cut down trees to block the game trails up out of there. He made a heavy log gate at the south end. There is a spring down in there. He told me wild horses have been watering there for many years. He told me it was a natural trap. He said someday he would show it to me, but now he never will. The arroyo is about half a mile north of where they made the second camp.'

Arch rocked back in his chair. If the posse riders had continued tracking they would have found where the outlaws had turned back. They hadn't and while he had felt unhappy about losing the fugitive as he gazed at the handsome 'breed woman he began feeling better.

She broke across his thoughts. 'I can take you there.'

He acknowledged the offer with a small smile. 'We'll find it,' he told her, 'you stay plumb away. Don't go skulkin' through the forest; if there's a fight you could get shot.' He stood up. 'I'll fetch you some supper. Stay in here, I'll be back shortly.'

She finally returned to the chair and sat. She had known about the settlement since childhood but this was her first visit and when Arch had said she'd had a long walk he had been right, but she had walked many times as far, in the mountains. She was physically strong and hardy.

Her problem had been to screw up enough courage to seek the settlement. It hadn't occurred to her that the constable might not be there when she arrived, and he hadn't, but she also had infinite patience. What had worried her was the possibility that someone searching for the constable might walk in. No one had. As she waited she decided she was both hungry and thirsty. There was an olla so she drank and when Arch returned with a dented tin tray with dishes of food on it, she accepted the tray and with averted eyes thanked him.

He told her the thanks was on the other foot. What she had done would give him another chance at catching the man who had bludgeoned her father and all the men who had stolen her father's horses.

While she was eating, the constable searched for Will Stanton and found him at the saloon. He also recruited burly Jim Meeker. He would have dragooned Timothy Farrel and his riders but they had left the settlement for home.

He needed another man; the rangemen he'd recruited from the countryside were also gone, and Josiah Parker wouldn't be able to make the ride.

He was ready to abandon the manhunt when the parson almost collided with Arch in front of the store. Arch took the parson to a nearby bench, sat down with him and explained he needed another posse rider and why. The shockle-headed minister looked wide-eyed. 'I've never ridden with a posse in my life,' he told the constable. 'You can find someone else. I wouldn't even know. . . .'

'You own a gun, don't you?' Arch asked, and when

the preacher nodded Arch said, 'Get it an' saddle up.
We'll be along for you directly.'

Before the preacher could speak again the constable was halfway in the direction of the rarely used,
dingy jailhouse.

Will Stanton was fresh when he tied up out front
of the log house with its stingy little barred front
window. He'd eaten like a horse, had slept and had
even borrowed the blacksmith's straight razor to
shave himself.

When he entered the log building he stopped
stone still. Arch was putting the tray of empty plates
aside. Abraham Carlyle's daughter looked even more
uncomfortable than the stockman did. Arch introduced them and explained why the woman was
there.

Stanton removed his hat with a flourish; although
he'd been gone quite a spell and had a wife miles
northward, he was still a male animal.

The last one to appear with a mount was the minister. He'd had to borrow one from a member of his
flock and although he had a shellbelt and holstered
Colt belted in place he wore a coat long enough to
conceal the fact that he was armed.

The difficulty was simply that the man he had
borrowed the horse from, out front of the saloon
where he could see congregating armed men down
in front of the log house, recognized the horse he'd
loaned and, even though the parson had his back to
the horse's owner and was wearing a coat, the
watcher had difficulty accepting the obvious fact that
the man of God was going to ride with a posse.

He did not see the 'breed woman. If she had been
visible he probably would have missed seeing her

anyway because before the riders got astride he had ducked back inside to tell the saloonman what he had seen, the Bible-banger riding with a posse, something which would stir folks up when the gossip spread.

7
Failure and Hope

Arch led off northward and left the road about where he'd left it before. It did not occur to him that his lack of success the other time might be duplicated, what did intrigue him was that the horsethieves had returned.

He speculated as he rode and decided the reason they had come back was, possibly, that with a large supply of horses, they would consider the risk worth the taking. By nature outlaws had to be gamblers.

It wouldn't be the army this time, not after what Arch had told the major, so it had to be another outlet for a sizeable band of horses. Probably Mexico.

He was rummaging his mind for answers when the parson came up beside him and said, 'From what Mister Stanton an' the others say, we're going after dangerous men, Constable.'

Arch was scanning the fading sun when he answered. 'You didn't know an old feller named Abraham Carlyle; they clubbed him to death so's they could run off his horses, which they sold to the army. We buried old Carlyle, you bein' along can say a prayer at the grave. Abraham deserves a proper send-off, Parson.'

They did not ride fast; as before Arch preferred reaching the uplands after sunset or a tad later.

When they encountered Carlyle's wagon ruts and rode over them on their right the heavily timbered country was already dark.

They were near enough to the small clearing where the log house stood when Muriel Carlyle appeared as she'd done before, out of nowhere like a ghost. The parson audibly gasped.

She approached Arch's left side, looked up and said, 'They rounded up horses. They have them in the trap. They must have done that while I was gone today.'

Arch told her to go home and stay there. She neither agreed nor disagreed but as the horsemen rode ahead she remained in the roadway.

Will Stanton told the constable the horsethieves were not wasting time. He thought the reason was that they wanted to make one last sashay, trap as many horses as they could and drive them out of the country.

Arch was watching for the trail they'd used before and did not comment. Will dropped back to explain his theory to the others until they were among forest giants and had to zigzag individually. When this occurred Stanton said no more. He'd have had to shout, something he wouldn't have done.

He had no idea where they were going but he was satisfied the outlaws they were hunting would hear a loud voice. In fact he thought it likely that the horsethieves would have sentinels out to watch and listen. It would have to be mostly listening because the dying day in open country had fully died in the timbered highlands hours earlier. Moving shadows would be noticeable even though their horses would make almost no noise; they were travelling over a springy carpeting of pine and fir needles centuries old. They muffled sound.

Arch aimed for the camp from which the horsethieves had fled and although he was confident of riding directly to it, in fact he required half an hour to find it.

From that place he had to guess, and when they passed the first camp, he told his companions what they were looking for and would have had them scatter if somewhere in the gloom a horse fight hadn't erupted.

They halted. Arch gestured for his companions to dismount and tie their horses. The minister had no carbine but as the others watched, he swept back the right side of his coat and tucked it under. Several glances were exchanged but no one commented.

Bert Fellows, the only rangeman, who wouldn't have been along if he hadn't been laid off when the riding season ended and who lived in the settlement, slouched up to the constable and spoke quietly. 'If they got 'em corralled, sure as hell they're close by. My guess is that they'll be in a hurry to bust out of the hills with this second bunch. I think, myself, they was crazy to come back.'

Arch nodded agreement without speaking. Pancho what-ever-his-name was, certainly was no greenhorn. He had stumbled on to a gold mine of horses which, to anyone accustomed to stealing anywhere from two to ten horses each raid, was the fulfilment of a dream. He'd killed Carlyle out of hand; his concern was the old man's horses gathered pretty much in one place for many years.

He had to come back, risk or no risk. He had to make one last quick gather and drive. He would do it in the night as he'd done it before. If the horse fight they had heard had come from inside the old man's horse trap, there could be little doubt but that Bert Fellow's surmise, like Arch's, was correct.

The horse fight ended as they usually did, as suddenly as it had started. They went in the direction of the noise slowly and warily. Somewhere in the night there were four renegades, possibly more but that wasn't likely. There had been five before the thin, weasel-eyed man had been set afoot.

They stopped stone still when a man sang out in Spanish. Whoever he was, his yell had sounded slightly north-easterly, the same direction they were advancing after listening to the horse fight.

Ranks of forest giants, many so old rot was eating away the heart-wood inside, made movement slow. So did caution.

The mountains had deep canyons, less deep arroyos and where pine and fir-needle resin did not sour the ground, there were massive, scraggly thickets of underbrush in places where sun reached, as high, and higher, than a man.

Arch picked up the sound of restless horses. He was altering the stalk slightly when a ghost glided into sight holding a hand aloft. They would have halted anyway, but the apparition made sure that they would.

Arch spoke quietly. 'I told you to go home an' stay there.'

Muriel Carlyle ignored that as she came closer and

raised an arm. 'They are going to open the gate.' She turned to lead the way without another word. The men with carbines wiped sweat and renewed their grips. Muriel abruptly went to the ground at the same time a dark outline palmed a belt-gun and moved in her direction. The parson faded behind a tree and kept stealthily sidling until he was south of the advancing horsethief. When he moved toward him the man caught movement from the corner of his eyes and whirled in a crouch. The only sound was of a six-gun being cocked. The parson spoke to the phantom in Spanish, 'Drop the pistol. I'll kill you. Drop the pistol!'

The phantom dropped his weapon.

Will Stanton approached the man, was close enough to make out a darkly stubbled face, bared teeth and flaming eyes as the man's left hand came forward with a knife held tightly.

Stanton stopped. 'Drop it,' he said in English. 'You damned fool there's guns all around you.'

The dark man snarled a reply. 'One shot and they'll be all around you!'

The preacher moved easterly, then back westerly. When he hit the crouched man facing Will Stanton the outlaw dropped his knife and went down with it.

They used the horsethief's bandanna, belt and tie-down thong to tie him.

When Muriel arose and gestured, they followed her. Bert Fellows dryly said, 'That's better; now there's only three of 'em.'

After Fellows spoke there was nothing more said as Muriel veered northward and the men followed. Where she emerged close to the drop-off of a dark place the men heard and saw horses. She told them the gate was southward at the lower end of the canyon. Where they were standing was on the west side of the arroyo. She had led them there confident that the horsethieves would be southward at the gate, and she was right. They could occasionally hear men speaking back and forth, sometimes in English, more often in Spanish.

She faced Arch when she said, 'They are ready to open the gate.'

He told Will and Bert, who had saddle guns, to seek targets and fire before the gate could be opened.

They were too far north to see moving men clearly, but when Stanton fired, his gunshot came moments before Bert Fellows fired and pandemonium broke loose. Men yelled in two languages; with nothing moving and badly impaired visibility, the horsethieves fired blind before they scattered.

The final yell was from a human with a deep voice yelling, '*Aviso!* They are many!'

Arch joined the firing. Will and the rangeman emptied their carbines and reloaded while the constable shot his six-gun empty. The lull was brief. When the scattered horsethieves paused they had muzzleblasts to aim at, but for both attackers and the attacked accurate firing was impossible.

Will abruptly called loudly. 'Bring up the others!'

The scattered firing from the area of the gate stopped. Someone spoke in English but not loudly. Arch picked up two words 'The horses', and correctly assuming someone was telling the horsethieves to get astride, led off southward in the direction of the gate.

The corralled horses were in turmoil, they ran blindly in the horse trap. Their noise made it impos-

sible for the possemen to pick up any sound of fleeing men. Arch was close enough to the massive log
gate to make out details when someone lightly
brushed his arm. He turned. Muriel Carlyle said,
'Follow me.'

They had little difficulty, she seemed to float
ahead of them, easily discernible. She moved swiftly,
the only time the men following her lost sight was
when huge old trees cut off sight of the woman, but
that lasted only moments.

They were nearing the most recent camp when
they heard the sound of desperate men on frightened horses in the darkness. Muriel moved more
rapidly, her followers did the same, but it was too
late. The horsethieves'd had too great a head start
and they had known where they were going. Their
variety of escape was dangerous, even if their mounts
hadn't been too terrified to avoid trees, their riders,
while less terrified, had only moments to rein around
forest giants before there was a collision, but they
managed.

Their escape was successful. Their pursuers
stopped only when the sounds of horses diminished
and ultimately faded altogether.

They returned to the camp before returning to
their own animals.

Arch was not hopeful as they snugged up and
swung astride. Bert Fellows the rangeman was
disgusted. As they moved cautiously in mounted
pursuit he said, 'We should've got closer.'

No one disputed that, in fact no one spoke as
Muriel, riding double with the constable, guided
them in territory she had grown up familiar with.
Only when they crossed a small clearing did she say,

'I wanted to open the gate, all those wild horses would have chased them.'

No one commented about that either. It was improbable that wild horses would have run down the horsethieves; they could have picked up their scent from a distance and whatever course they might have taken, they would have changed it.

By the time they got to the Carlyle cabin the darkness was turning increasingly chilly. Muriel slid to the ground, looked up and said, 'They won't come back,' and Arch nodded. He believed she was right.

The ride back to Cold Spring was made by dispirited men on hungry horses.

It was late when they rode into the settlement, there might have been a light or two but they noticed none. Out front of the smithy where they dismounted, the parson spoke aside to the constable. 'They will be south of the border by tomorrow,' and Arch nodded. It was no consolation that the horsethieves would not be driving horses.

This time when the constable offered to share his lean-to with Will Stanton the cowman accepted.

After the animals had been cared for and the unhappy posse riders had gone home, the constable fired up his cook stove and went to work preparing a meal. He had no idea what time it was, if he'd known he might have waited another hour or so when the caféman lighted a lamp and fired up his cook stove.

Will Stanton fell asleep in a chair. Arch roused him to eat. Neither man spoke until their plates were empty then the stockman said, 'Well hell; that ends it.' The constable removed the dishes when he replied, 'They won't come back, that's a fact.' He smiled tiredly. 'They was within an ace of chousin' the horses out of the corral like they done last time. I'd guess they'll never again come so close.' Arch pointed to a bunk built against the east wall.

As Stanton went there and sat down to kick off his boots someone knocked lightly but insistently on the roadway door. The men exchanged a look. Stanton stood up as Arch started through the store. Stanton followed with his right hand behind his back. When Arch opened the door and saw the old man's daughter, he was speechless. She couldn't possibly spend what remained of the night in his living-quarters.

She stopped his heart for two seconds when she spoke. 'They went back.'

Stanton came closer still with his right hand out of sight. 'They?'

The woman barely more than acknowledged the stockman. Her attention was on the store-keeping constable. 'I was out back of my father's log house. I heard riders and hid in an arroyo. There were three of them going north.'

'Did you recognize them?' Arch asked.

'Not the men, no, but I knew their horses.'

Stanton stifled a curse before speaking. 'Arch, that's what they did before, went south then turned back.'

The constable took Muriel by the arm, relighted the lamp and stood her by the stove as he asked his first question.

'Are you sure, Muriel?'

'I am certain,' she replied looking at him without blinking. She added a little more. 'They know they was chased. Maybe they even know you came back here.'

Stanton sat on the edge of his bunk regarding the

woman as he addressed the constable. 'They was ready to open the gate. If they go back that's all they got to do. Open the gate an' try to keep the horses in sight. They'll lose some; it's dark an' worse in that timbered country. But how long'll it take them to ride up there, lean from the saddle, open the gate and chouse the old man's horses out? Minutes. Even if we was up there they could get the horses running south before we could catch up.'

Arch got Muriel a cup of coffee. She thanked him and put the cup aside. She'd tasted black java before. Those other times she had told her father coffee would never replace spring water.

Arch offered to feed her. She rummaged her clothing and produced several gnarled, dark sticks of jerky, and smiled. As she was stowing the jerky she said, 'You can't get up there in time. When I saw them pass like ghosts in the night, the moon was hanging on the rims. It is gone now.'

Stanton went to refill his cup and instead of returning to the bunk he sat at the table warming his hands by curling them around the cup. He looked at Arch and waited.

The constable also got a refill but he drank the coffee. Muriel watched with something close to admiration; coffee smelled wonderful. It tasted terrible.

Arch straightened up slowly. 'If they come south with the drive like they done last time. . . .'

'What if they do?' the stockman asked.

'Roust up the whole settlement, string 'em out with guns. When they hear horses comin' start shootin' high. Wild horses get scairt easy; they'll likely scatter in every direction.'

Stanton drained his cup, which allowed him time

to think. As he lowered the cup he said, 'If you can roust 'em up, an' if they'll go out there with guns . . . Arch, someone could get hurt. Maybe killed.'

Arch didn't think so. He knew something about wild horses; they ran blind when they were terrorized, some would run back the way they had come. They had a homing instinct, but even if they lacked it they would never stampede in the direction of the visible muzzleblast of guns and their accompanying noise.

When he explained this to the stockman and the handsome woman neither broke the ensuing silence until Muriel said, 'Can you get the people ready? By now they've had time to get the horses running.'

Stanton had something to say that kept the constable quiet. 'They might make their stampede in a different direction. They sure-Lord aren't goin' to sell more animals to the army.'

Arch sat at the table near the smoking lantern whose wick hadn't been trimmed. To Muriel his profile looked harsh, almost evil. He finally spoke, looking at the stockman.

'Messico, Mister Stanton. Not Fort Buchanan, Messico. They got a clean run the whole distance an' over the border into Chihuahua.'

Stanton considered and shrugged. He wasn't convinced, but for a fact the border was fairly close and once over the line not even *norteamericano* soldiers could pursue horsethieves. He stood up, yawned prodigiously, stretched and looked at the 'breed daughter of the old man who, dead or not, was the basic source of all this. He said, 'They don't know me nor her, Constable.'

Arch nodded and started for the nearest door,

which was the only one in his lean-to. It opened into the alley on the west side of the settlement. He paused briefly to say, 'Muriel, stay in here,' and sighed because he'd given this order before and she hadn't obeyed. He looked at Stanton. 'Give me half an hour.' Then he closed the door after himself.

Stanton gazed at the woman, wagging his head in strong silence. She evidently did not share his doubts because she told him that the constable was a good man, and he was known. She had faith in what he had embarked upon.

Stanton did not disagree. In fact he said nothing as he eyed the bunk with a woeful expression.

Outside, dogs barked and once a mule brayed. There was no sound west of the Missouri River more raucous, downright ugly and discordant than the braying of a mule.

Stanton checked his weapons. Muriel watched him without expression. When he was satisfied and had placed his Winchester on the table she startled him with a blandly asked question.

'Why doesn't he have a woman?'

Stanton cleared his throat, moved to shove a scantling into the stove and replied as he straightened around. 'For all I know, he does have,' he replied, and instantly knew he had said the wrong thing.

Muriel looked away from Stanton and, without expression, her dark gaze fixed on the far wall.

8
Men and Animals

The fate that hadn't done well by the constable of late may have had a change of heart, because when Arch left his lean-to there was a gunmetal grey sky and a hint of golden brilliance below the furthest curve of the horizon.

Cold Spring was coming to life, smoke from breakfast fires made dark plumes above stove pipes, men and their dogs were choring, hungry animals made noise and a particular Rhode Island Red rooster with powerful lungs and a terrible voice, crowed from a tree perch somewhere on the east side of the settlement.

Arch'd had misgivings before leaving his lean-to about getting folks out of bed. He still had misgivings when he approached a large man wearing black suspenders who nodded and leaned on his three-tined hay fork as he said, 'Mornin' to you, Constable. They tell me you been busier'n a rutting buck lately.'

Arch smiled, conscious of dark-rimmed eyes and beard stubble as he began explaining why he was in the man's yard.

The householder listened with no interruption

and no expression until Arch finished, then he leaned the fork aside and said, 'I'll tell Momma an' meet you in front of the store as soon as I get my guns.'

Arch saw other people, except for one, whose wife refused to allow the constable to see her husband because he was flat down with summer complaint. Arch was successful. Down at the forge Jim Meeker eyed the constable owlishly while tying his shoeing apron into place and said, 'You got to give 'em credit, Arch. They're what my pa used to call real perservering.' Meeker paused to methodically untie the apron, toss it aside and say, 'How many'll there be with the Carlyle horses?'

'Maybe three, no more'n four.'

Meeker had another question. 'How many folks you got dragooned so far?'

'Thirteen.'

'I'll make fourteen. It wouldn't set well goin' out there with thirteen, it's a bad number. I'll be up in front of the store as soon as I can.'

An odd thing about widow-women; how they did it was anyone's guess but Mary Elkins had unlocked the store and was waiting when the townsmen began congregating. At first she simply wondered but as more arrived, all armed to the gills, she asked the blacksmith just what in hell was going on. He told her tersely as he watched the preacher coming down the centre of the road. The dowdy woman made a sour comment. 'Any rangemen coming, because what you're talkin' about could mean a lot of men got to be strung out.' She paused as the minister arrived, looked from his Winchester to the bulge under his coat, and also said, 'You stampede wild horses and some of 'em will sure as hell enter the settlement.'

Jim Meeker offered a growled remark. 'Tell the womenfolk to keep their kids inside.'

Before Mary Elkins could ask how she could do that and mind the store the blacksmith walked over to meet the minister. The other men eyed the holy man askance. But whatever their thoughts they kept them to themselves.

Arch arrived with Will Stanton. Meeker nodded; it wasn't thirteen it was fifteen, a more acceptable number; thirteen of anything, money, marbles or chalk, was an unlucky number.

There were lights, about twice as many as normally showed around breakfast time. No one commented but for a fact if drivers pushing a large band of stolen horses weren't blind they'd be entitled to wonder about so much lamplight.

But eventually enough candles and less lamps were doused until the settlement looked normal as Arch led the way westerly and only halted where the tracks of the earlier drive were visible. It was cold; the men were bundled into coats, some wore gloves which they pocketed as Arch deployed them across the full width of the old tracks, and further.

There was cover, an occasional tree, mostly thickets of sage and thornpin. When the constable and Will Stanton positioned the last man as far westerly as Arch thought would be necessary and were walking back, Stanton said, 'It'll be daylight directly,' and Arch nodded. As he walked toward the centre of the line he concentrated on looking northward. It bothered him that the other drive had been made in darkness; this time given an hour or so there would be daylight.

Stanton put the constable's increasing anxiety into words, 'Suppose they went in some other direction.'

Arch did not answer because a distant blinding flash of reflected light struck his face. Again Will Stanton made a guess. 'Would that be the 'breed woman signallin' us?'

Arch hoped very hard Stanton was right, but as far as he could see there was neither movement nor dust. The sun was still an hour or so from completely clearing the horizon but the predawn made fair visibility.

A lanky man arose from behind a bush with a maple-stocked, fragile-looking Kentucky rifle in his hand. He said, 'Constable, put your ear to the ground.'

Both Stanton and Trumbull got down and remained that way until the tall man from Cold Spring said, 'You hear it?'

They arose nodding. The reverberation of many running horses was audible. The man with the Kentucky rifle disappeared behind his bush.

Someone to the west whistled and gestured with an upraised carbine. Among the older men who saw this gesture memories came; that was how broncos *ozyu we tawatas* brandished their weapons before an attack.

Will got down a second time and almost immediately arose, turned and squinted into the predawn distance. 'Ought to be able to see 'em,' he muttered to himself. Moments later that Winchester-waving individual, young and eager, yelled that they were coming. Arch still saw no movement, neither did most of the others but they strained.

The distance was still several miles and by the time

it was possible to discern a distant blur of movement, the sun still hadn't risen far enough to help visibility very much.

Several women came out carrying carbines and rifles. In exasperation the blacksmith met them and with no tact told them forcibly to go back, they weren't needed. Several did turn back but three burly women, large boned, muscular and adamant told Meeker to go to hell, and pushed past seeking their men among the hidden settlement's long line of stiffly waiting men.

Meeker started for the constable. An old man growled surlily at him from cover. 'Ya danged idiot, they get much closer an' they'll see you. Get the hell to ground.'

The horse-trading blacksmith turned aside and faded from sight on the downside of a tree.

Arch and Will Stanton waited until they saw horses and dust. They were unable to see drovers who would be on both sides and in the drag where the dust was thickest. As they sought cover Stanton repeated what he'd said before. 'They're crazy to come the same way.'

Arch nodded but said, 'They weren't bothered before.'

'Well hell, that was a surprise.'

A concealed man spoke gruffly. 'They got a reason. I don't recollect ever meetin' a cowman who could read minds.'

Arch glanced down the westerly line where the settlement men – and three women – were waiting. Except for puny reflection of an occasional rifle barrel his concealed companions were adequately hidden. He sank to one knee on the downward side of a tree and leaned on his carbine. He had never been in combat but now he understood what it would have been like.

Will also knelt waiting. That dazzling flash of distant light wavered again twice then no more. Arch was diverted only long enough to make a bleak smile. However this ended, when it was over he would ride back up there. The 'breed daughter of the old man had clearly inherited his grit, to the extent that being told to stay in his lean-to, she obviously had done as she had done before – behaved as she wanted to not as she had been told to.

The oncoming horses were running without deviating, unusual for wild horses. Tame horses would have acted the same way but providing they had a leader on horseback to follow. What had probably happened was that some animals had strayed before the band left the forested uplands, the remaining horses, with two flankers and a drag rider ran freely due southward.

When they were close enough – within rifle-shot in fact – for the hiding ambushers to make out individual animals, one in particular stood out. He was tall, about sixteen hands, had a wavy mane, a sleek bay coat and was high-headed. He was the leader. It was possible he was a stallion but he could just as easily have been a ridgling; the two temperaments were identical. The physical difference was that while stallions could 'catch' a mare, ridglings could not.

Arch admired the tall bay. As the band swept closer he wasn't the only admirer. Jim Meeker was more intrigued by the high-headed horse than he was in a rider who appeared out of the dust.

Arch raised his carbine. Other guns were snugged

back. When the wing rider raised his quirt to strike his mount Arch fired, all along the strung out line of intercepting villagers gunfire erupted. To wild horses it made no difference whether the hidden shooters aimed over their heads or at their hearts, they jammed to a sliding halt and in less than two seconds were either turning back or breaking away easterly and westerly.

The gunfire continued, dust arose, men yelled, the wing-rider Arch had seen palmed a six-gun and fired wildly at the muzzleblasts scarcely discernible through the dust.

Someone lowered his sights. The wing-rider was punched backwards, his grip on the reins tightened until the horse reared. The man fell off.

Through the pandemonium someone screamed in Spanish. Will Stanton stood up seeking whoever had yelled. He had a ghostly target but at the moment he fired Arch yanked him violently down.

The horsethieves fired back but as the concealed villagers continued to fire high the return fire ended; the horsethieves were riding for their lives trying to get wide or to stay ahead of the blindly running horses. Too many men to count had been trampled to death beneath the feet of blind-running horses and cattle.

The engagement did not last more than ten minutes. When it was over and people appeared from places of concealment, they could scarcely see their closest companion for dust.

Will wrapped a bandanna across his lower face. Others did the same as the sound of horses fleeing back the way they had come diminished.

Someone about a mile easterly at the settlement

blew a bugle. The ambushers listened and several wagged their heads. The father of a bachelor who lived near the church had come out of the War Between The States with at least half of his marbles missing. His son cared for him very well, but every now and then the old soldier would hear something that agitated him, like gunfire, would rummage for his dented old bugle and blow it. No one knew what the bugle calls meant but the deranged old soldier knew. They meant, Charge! Charge!

Arch hunted for the horsethief who had been shot off his horse. Mostly, the others milled and muttered, some struck out for the settlement.

What Arch found was a dark-skinned man with pale-blue eyes sitting up trying to straighten a leg which was twisted beneath him. The parson appeared. They stood watching the horsethief. The parson knelt to help straighten the broken leg. The blue-eyed Mexican's six-gun was close by. He made no movement to retrieve it. The preacher tried Spanish and the horsethief replied in English. 'I fell on it. I heard it snap. It's painful, Father.' He looked up at the constable and said, 'Shoot me. What are you waiting for?'

Arch leaned, retrieved the handgun, shoved it into the front of his britches and asked the minister to stay with the prisoner while he searched for others.

The sun began its ponderous climb, warmth eventually arrived. The blacksmith caught the injured horsethief's animal and struck out for the settlement leading it.

The minister rocked back on his heels regarding the horsethief. He said in Spanish, 'Your name is what?' and got an answer in English. 'Jésus Quiroz y

Teran. What is your name?'

Although the preacher had spent years in the south-west he still had difficulty with a somewhat common custom of children being named Jesus, even though among Spanish-speakers it was pronounced to sound like 'Hay, sus'.

He answered the blue-eyed man's question after a slight delay. 'My name is Wilber Stocker. I am the minister in that settlement yonder, the Baptist minister.' He looked upward and addressed the constable. 'I need two stout sticks to splint his leg until we can get him back to the settlement.'

Arch walked away. Finding deadfalls among the underbrush was not difficult, but it was the nature of sage and thornpin not to have straight limbs.

A large, masculine woman carrying a saddle gun and with a holstered revolver around her middle, asked what Arch was looking for and when he told her she looked coldly at him. 'Shoot the son of a bitch,' she said, and walked firmly in the direction of Cold Spring.

He found two sticks neither of which was really straight but were not too crooked either.

When he got back where the preacher and the horsethief were conversing in Spanish, the minister went to work splinting the broken leg, which was difficult to do because the horsethief also had a slight gunshot wound in the same leg. He did not once look up. He knew how painful it was; he did not want to see agony reflected in the horsethief's face.

Will Stanton who had gone to the village, returned with a bottle from Joe Parker's place. The horsethief thanked Will and drank deeply before returning the bottle as he considered both Stanton and the constable and said, '*Muerta en la hora.*'

It was a statement not a question and while the
constable and the stockman looked blankly back the
preacher said, 'No. There will be no hanging.'

They got the injured man to his feet and, with the
minister on one side, the constable on the other,
started for the settlement, which was a considerable
distance. Will thought they should have borrowed a
wagon but said nothing as he walked back with them.

The pain was excruciating, something that showed
in the locked jaw and the beads of sweat on the
horsethief's face.

By the time they got him to the settlement Mary
Elkins was waiting at the store with a clean quilt
spread on the floor. She did not like Mexicans, for
whatever reason, so she stood primly as they lowered
the blue-eyed man to the quilt. Arch growled at curious people who had entered the store and the timid
ones retreated as far as the doorway.

He cleared out the others and there was some
mumbling as the store was emptied, only those
crowding at the doorway remained.

The gossip was already inevitably starting, and Joe
Parker's saloon seethed with it. Some fantastic stories
emerged from the wonderful fumes of Joe's bar and
Joe, with one arm in a sling made of two red bandan-
nas, did nothing to discourage anything, not even
the ultimate growling which concluded in a suggestion for hanging. It was all good for business and in
a place no larger than Cold Spring a merchant had
to do everything he could imagine to keep the pleats
out of his stomach.

At the minister's insistence they moved the
horsethief to the parsonage, a small house on the

east side of the church where, because the preacher was unmarried, there was enough space.

Arch went to his lean-to to wash down and rest. Will Stanton did not appear which was a blessing; the constable was dog-tired and exhausted. He slept like the dead, did not awaken until shortly before daylight of the following day, hungry as a nursing mother.

At the eatery, because he arrived hours after the regulars had dined and departed, he had the counter to himself. The caféman leaned opposite the counter, arms folded, regarding the constable in stony silence. He did not even speak when he got Arch a refill for his coffee cup and before the constable finished, the uncouth, sullen man had returned to his cooking area shielded from view by a large rug of some kind that had seen better days.

Up at the parsonage Will Stanton, Jim Meeker and Mary Elkins were in the room with the parson. The dowdy woman looked up and said, 'I locked the store,' and went back to work with the blacksmith's help cleaning and bandaging the wound and resplinting and wrapping the blue-eyed man's broken leg. He said something to the minister in Spanish and Mary Elkins flared up at him. 'Damned greaser, use English, if you know it. When's the last time you had a bath! You smell like hell!'

The horsethief regarded the woman for a moment, then forced a sweaty smile in the direction of the constable, and spoke in English. 'It was a good ambush,' he said.

Arch did not acknowledge the compliment, instead he said, 'Where'll Pancho Jefferson go now?'

The horsethief's expression subtly changed.

'Jefferson? His name is Pancho Allende. Jefferson?'

'We caught a wiry, weasel-eyed man. He said his name was Jefferson. Where will Allende go now?'

'I don't know. We were goin' to take those horses to Mexico. Maybe he's gone down there.'

'There was three of you. Allende, you'n one other.'

'Jaime Ortega. He will go to Mexico. He wanted to leave when we sold the first herd to the soldiers. He has a wife in Chihuahua.'

Mary Elkins straightened and flinched. She brushed grey hair clear of her face with the back of one hand, looked across at Jim Meeker and said, 'That'll do.' She lowered her gaze to the horsethief. 'A man don't need two legs for a hangin'.'

She left the parsonage on her way to the store. She was accosted several times and brushed aside the questions except to say, 'He talks English real good, for a beaner.'

At the store, customers came to ask questions not to buy. When she tired of it she shooed them out, locked the store and headed home. She was in the process of scrubbing when Tim Farrel arrived. She met him at the door, told him what had happened and didn't get a chance to close the door on him, Farrel left her standing there on his way to the parsonage.

Later, when Arch and the stockman went to the constable's lean-to and emptied two shot glasses, Stanton said, 'I'm goin' up there in the mornin', pick out ten horses, take 'em down to the fort an' trade 'em for my ten head. You got any objections?'

'Only one,' the constable replied dryly. 'If you take ten horses from up yonder you'll be horse stealin'.'

Stanton cocked his head slightly. 'You'll come after me,' he asked, 'after all I done with you an' these settlement folks?'

Arch considered the stockman over a long silent moment then said, 'I'll ride up there with you,' and arose to leave the room by the alley door to pee.

9
A New Day

Arch took an all-over bath, shaved and laid out clean clothes before bedding down. Come daybreak he lay awake wondering whether it would be a good idea to leave Cold Spring when its mood was in favour of a hanging.

He dressed, went down to the eatery, met Will Stanton and told the north-country stockman he had a chore to do before he'd be ready to ride.

He went up to the parsonage, declined the preacher's offer to see the horsethief and told the minister he had to leave for the day and would leave the horsethief in the preacher's care.

He mentioned the lynch talk and was prepared to suggest that Joe Parker and maybe the blacksmith could be induced to sit with the minister until Arch got back.

The parson smiled. 'I'll handle it, Constable.'

Arch found Will out front of the store with a horse he'd hired from Jim Meeker. They left town riding stirrup and because it was past sun-up people saw them leave, which meant speculation would begin before they were out of sight.

Stanton mentioned the heliograph and Arch replied that was his reason for riding up yonder; to thank the old man's daughter for flashing the signal which warned them the drive had left the uplands.

Stanton rode a hundred yards before he spoke. 'Right handsome woman, Constable.'

Arch agreed by nodding without speaking.

Stanton persisted. 'A man could do a heap worse, an' she'll own the old man's ranch.'

This time the constable put a cold gaze on his companion. 'If you're talkin' about yourself, you already got a woman. If you're talkin' about me, I'll tell you what my pappy told me many years ago: if a man wants to live long he won't get personal with folks.'

The rest of the ride was made in silence, only when they had the log house in sight did one of them speak again. Arch said, 'I figured she'd be here.'

Stanton's reply was logical. 'She'll be somewhere close by.'

Arch led off north-easterly among big trees. There was an old path to follow but in places it wasn't clear; moccasins didn't make much of an imprint.

They didn't have to go far. In fact they had halted at one of those places where the sign was almost indistinguishable and Stanton said, 'You go on, I'll go to the corral and pick out ten horses.'

The constable turned in the saddle to speak when Abraham Carlyle's daughter appeared from among forest gloom. She said, 'Good morning. Did you see my light?'

Arch nodded. 'Saw it twice.'

'It meant they were starting their drive. Did it help?'

'It helped a lot,' Arch told the handsome woman.

'I guessed it did because most of the horses came back. I saw them coming and watched them get among the trees. They would want to find their friends and grass.'

She turned her attention to Will Stanton. 'Now you can go home.'

Will fidgeted, hung fire for a long moment and Arch spoke. 'He's shy ten horses they sold to the army. He wants 'em back.'

She asked a naïve question. 'Will they give them back?'

Arch shook his head. 'Not likely.'

Muriel Carlyle gazed thoughtfully at the stockman for a moment before speaking. 'Some of the horses will go back inside the trap. My father salted them in there. Go close the gate and find ten you like.'

'For how much?' Stanton asked.

She smiled. 'For helping the constable, nothing.'

Will looked from one to the other, fidgeted briefly then told Arch he would meet him at the old man's house and rode in the direction of the corral.

Arch dismounted. The woman led the way to her log house in a stumped-over clearing from which had come the logs, and showed him the small lean-to where he could leave his horse and pitch wild-oat hay to it.

Inside the log house, daylight appeared on a slanting tangent. There were two glass windows, the most expensive and difficult things to find in the Cold Spring territory.

The furniture had been made by someone who was adept with hands and tools. There was a gun rack holding a shotgun, a rifle and a carbine. The stone fireplace showed considerable use. Altogether the house, smaller than the Carlyle house, was comfortable and pleasant.

The woman made herb tea which she had been raised on and showed him a faded tintype of her mother, a handsome woman from whom the daughter had inherited more than just looks, she had also inherited the strong physique.

In her own world she seemed at ease, she talked and smiled, even laughed when Arch tasted the tea and put the cup aside. She was interested in what had happened at the settlement and when he explained what had been done she looked him straight in the eye and said, 'You are a wise man.'

He doubted that but did not speak for a while and when he did he changed the subject, explained more fully what had happened to Will Stanton's horses. She made a slight gesture when she said, 'There are many horses. He can find ten he likes.'

Arch didn't doubt that, he had doubts about Stanton abandoning the horses bearing his brand. From what he had learned during their acquaintanceship Will Stanton was a stubborn man.

She stirred life into coals in the stove and prepared a meal. Arch relaxed, the woman seemed either trained to show no emotion or unwilling for him to see her emotions. The constable was the first man, excluding her father, she had invited into her home. If she was conscious of this she gave no indication.

She was a good cook. Both her parents had told her that men were meat eaters. How she managed to store meat the constable would not understand for a long time.

The sun was slanting away when Will Stanton appeared. He told them he had found ten animals he liked at the salt lick. One was a tall, high-headed dark bay with a wavy mane. Arch remembered the horse.

The woman fed Will and afterwards they visited until the sun was beginning to get low enough to be lost beyond the giant trees. She went out and watched them get ready to ride. They thanked her and headed back the way they had come. The woman stood like a statue watching until they passed from sight.

She returned to the house to clean dishes, kindle a fire in the stone fireplace, and to go out for a walk. She went to a windswept rocky place which, throughout her childhood, had been her vantage point from where she could see almost as far as the settlement. On dark nights she could make out pinpricks of light that far distant. She had thought as a child she was looking at the world of settled people; except from books her father brought, she had no idea of any larger world.

Arch and Will rode in silence almost until they reached the stage road, then Stanton mentioned the horses he had liked and in the next breath said something that did not surprise the constable. He said, 'The army's got no right to keep my horses.'

Arch was tempted to mention the bill-of-sale but refrained as they entered the village where Arch unlocked the store and went through to his living area while Will returned his animal to its owner down at the smithy.

In the morning the parson came to the store to say it had required the threat of his shotgun to deter several men from taking the horsethief to the local hang tree. The parson did not mention names and Arch did not ask for any.

Later in the day he went up to visit the horsethief.

Except for the flourishing dark beginning of a beard the horsethief seemed no different. He mentioned men coming to hang him and smiled about the minister using his shotgun to discourage them. He also said, 'But they will be back.'

Arch did not agree but let that pass. He wanted to know more about the man with two names, one *gringo*, one Mexican.

Quiroz y Teran was easy to talk to and was a good conversationalist. He told of meeting Allende in a place called San Antonio de las Flores, a mining community and had joined Allende because mining was unpleasant work and being paid was something mine owners seemed to forget from time to time.

He told of raiding in Mexico, so many times and so many places that the government put a reward on the head, alive or dead, of anyone who rode with Pancho Allende.

'And that was when he came up into the *Estados Unidos* to steal cattle and horses, and to rob when we could. There may even be rewards out for us up here too, *quien sabe?* I was with Pancho when he found the rancho with the good horses in a corral. Ten of them. We drove them all night through terrible country. Pancho already knew of the old man, Carlyle, so we drove the horses there and put them in a big corral. Then Pancho and Flores, that skinny one you said you caught, he went with Pancho to kill the old man.'

Arch dryly interrupted. 'No way to prove it was them, they're gone. Safe to say it was them.'

The blue gaze of Quiroz y Teran did not waver. 'Listen to me, *gringo*, so far I don't lie to you. You want me to tell the truth, don't try to put words in my mouth.'

They traded a long stare before the horsethief resumed speaking. 'This much I can tell you about Pancho Allende. He was one of eleven children. They all died but Pancho and one sister. She was sold to an *hacendado*. Pancho could never find her. No one knew the rich man's name.

'His father stole two chickens to feed his family. The *rurales* came and shot him in his dooryard. Two chickens!'

Quiroz y Teran's eyes strayed and returned. 'He killed *rurales* wherever he found them, so the reward got larger. You understand?'

Arch nodded without speaking.

'We came up here. It was easier. When we found that old man with all those horses. . . .' The horsethief rolled his eyes heavenward. 'It was a gift from God.'

Arch lifted his hat, scratched and reset the hat. 'Before you found the old man with all the horses. . . ?'

'We robbed stages, ran cattle below the border and sold them. We robbed isolated ranches.'

'And murdered folks,' Arch said quietly.

Quiroz y Teran considered the constable for a moment before resuming his story. 'Listen to me,' he said quietly, blue gaze fixed on the constable. 'When no one wants you in this life, when no one cares what happens to you, when no one will give you work – tell me, *condestable*, what do you do?'

Arch said, 'Steal horses,' and they both laughed.

Arch stood up. 'Tell me about Quiroz y Teran, *ojo claros.*'

The man with the rigid, bandaged leg looked steadily at Arch for a long time before saying, 'A fool, friend. An idiot. My father was Alfred Taylor, a mine owner. When he married my mother he renamed himself Quiroz, and I his son had blue eyes. I ran away from a *Catolico* school. The rest you can imagine. Aguardiente, tequila, even mezcal. I fought because of the blue eyes. . . . I told you about meeting Pancho Allende. You can guess the rest. And now, Constable, they will hang me.' He slid his gaze to the far wall and spoke softly. 'I was to marry; she ran away and I couldn't find her, until in a mountain village they showed me her grave.' The blue eyes returned to Arch's face. 'Maybe now I will find her.'

Arch left the parsonage with evening coming. He ate at the café and went to his lean-to in back of the store. When Will Stanton knocked on the alley door he admitted him. Stanton had eaten and now considered the constable as he said, 'You look like you just lost your last friend.'

Arch sat on a bench. 'I sat a spell with the horsethief,' he said and the stockman erupted with venom. 'I heard the preacher used a shotgun so's folks couldn't hang the son of a bitch.'

Arch changed the subject. 'You can trail those horses the old man's girl gave you. No need to stay any longer.'

That sparked another eruption. 'I want *my* horses! It was decent of her to offer me the other ones, but it's not the same.'

Arch blew out a long sigh, went to the stove for a cup of coffee and while his back was to the stockman he said, 'You're welcome to bed down here if you want to.'

For Will Stanton it wasn't so much the two bits Meeker charged as it was the inconvenience of getting rid of chaff in the morning that encouraged him to say, 'Thanks.'

Stanton was one of those individuals who could sleep through the Second Coming, golden trumpets and all, but the constable required longer to get to sleep. There was something about the old man's daughter that bothered him. He had seen, had even known, his share of women; none had ever bothered him as did Muriel Carlyle. Before falling asleep he had a clear vision of her smiling at him in her log house.

In the morning while he was out back cleaning up and shaving, someone came out back and beat on the door. He opened it with half a lathered face and the saloonman stood there with his arm in its red bandanna sling. He said, 'The son of a bitch escaped in the night.'

Arch didn't ask who the 'son of a bitch' was. He asked how the horsethief had done it with one leg splinted and rigid. The answer he got was bluntly given.

'In a buggy, for Chris'sake,' and, at the blank look he got, Parker also said, 'A Jim Meeker rig, one of 'em he's got parked out back. Buggy, horse, harness an' all. Jim's back-trackin'. Seems whoever got the bastard done it long after dark, went up the alley to the parsonage an' got him, busted leg an' all. The parson didn't hear a thing.'

Arch used a towel to wipe soap off his face, shouldered past the saloonman, returned to the lean-to

for his shellbelt and holstered Colt. Parker followed
him, talking a mile a minute.

'He didn't do it himself. Jim said it could have
been someone from the settlement.'

Arch finished dressing and arming himself and led
off through the store to the roadway. Daylight had
arrived. He asked if Joe had seen Will Stanton and
got a negative head wag.

Stanton emerged from the eatery chewing on a
toothpick. He was startled at the thrusting no-
nonsense approach of Joe Parker and the constable,
and got rid of the toothpick as Arch told him of the
crisis. Stanton might have spoken but the horse trading blacksmith came up and said, 'Went up the west
side alley, parked behind the parsonage, got inside
and helped the bastard leave the house, get into the
rig and they went arrer-straight for the border.'

Arch said, 'You're sure?' And got a sour look from
Meeker. 'Constable, that's my top buggy. I'd know its
track anywhere. The near side front wheel didn't
shrink enough when I sweated on a new tyre, so I
drilled it and bolted it. Every turn of that wheel
leaves the bolt-head mark.'

Arch addressed the stockman. 'Get your horse.'
After Stanton had departed Joe Parker said, 'Never
was a buggy made that could out-distance a saddle
animal,' and Jim Meeker offered a dry contradiction.
'Depends on how much head start they got.
Constable, you want me to ride along?'

Arch declined the offer. Jim Meeker was a hot-
tempered individual. He had lost a horse and a
buggy and wouldn't be an ideal companion in a hunt
for them.

As he and Will left town by the south roadway the

stockman asked if Arch had eaten. He hadn't, and for the moment he felt no hunger. Instead of replying to the question he asked one of his own. 'Who in hell would want Quiroz that bad?'

Stanton answered quickly. 'His companero, Pancho whatever-his-name is.'

'In a damned buggy, Will?'

'Quiroz couldn't straddle a horse, could he?'

Because it was early and also because the usual tracks were made by wagons not buggies, following the sign was not difficult. They loped when they could. Meeker's comment about a head start was in the constable's mind.

The south road heading toward Glorioso was straight and the land was flat. They had been riding for two hours when Arch scratched his head as he said, 'We might catch sight of 'em directly.'

They didn't catch sight of them but they caught sight of something else: Jim Meeker's abandoned buggy with the harness animal asleep about a hundred yards on the west side of the road. They saw where the tracks led in that direction about the same time they saw the rig.

As Will was dismounting, he ignored the harnessed animal as well as the buggy to quarter like a hunting dog. While Arch was examining the buggy Stanton called to him.

It wasn't just several sets of boot imprints that intrigued the constable and his companion, it was the clear rowel marks, the kind only Chihuahua spurs made with their oversized rowels. The only riders who wore Chihuahua spurs were Mexicans. Part of the reason Chihuahua rowels made clear imprints was because Mexicans rarely wore boots, they wore shoes.

Arch stood gazing southward, the direction several mounted men had ridden, and shook his head. 'Quiroz can't stand that for long,' he said, heading for his saddle animal.

It wouldn't hurt the harnessed animal to stand out there for a while. It was possible that despite the constable's refusal to have the blacksmith ride with him, Meeker would take up the trail alone, in which case he'd find his rig and horse.

There were three of them and it was easy to see from the tracks that they were not making good time, which obviously would be because of the horsethief with the rigid leg.

Stanton thought they would be trying to reach Glorioso, where he had never been but of which he had heard about.

Arch did not contradict the stockman, but the distance between Cold Spring and Glorioso was sixty miles, a greater distance than even coach passengers could cover in one day. He thought the men they were tracking would not enter Glorioso, not with one of them riding with a splinted and bandaged leg, something guaranteed to attract attention, and he was right, the tracks left the stage road about four miles from the abandoned buggy and went westerly.

It was easier to read sign after the tracks left the road because there were no other tracks in a vast expanse of semi-desert country, but they were still riding when the sun began to redden as it moved closer to some very distant mountains which were heat-hazed to the extent that it was difficult to make them out.

Stanton, who did not know the country, swore

aloud. As far as he could see there was nothing but distantly undulating rangeland, empty of any kind of movement.

There were occasional trees, but they weren't the large firs and pines of the northerly country, they were spindly little paloverdes, their shade was minimal and while to someone appreciative of fragile beauty they would be something to marvel about and remember, to the inhabitants of the country where they grew, as well as to manhunters, they scarcely earned a second glance.

The land itself was clearly a territory of little rain. It was, in its own way, amazingly different from the Cold Spring country, it was instead a uniform colour of bleached tan. It had scraggly underbrush but only in scattered places and if the manhunters had cared to look they would have noticed that animals had browsed off much of the brush. This was sheep country. It was even more goat country, but they saw neither as they followed the tracks of three horsemen. There were wide arroyos, some large enough to contain a settlement as large as Cold Spring with land left over. These arroyos, products of prehistoric floods occasionally had springs around which trees and grass grew, but unless the trees were tall their tops did not show to interrupt the appearance of flatness.

Only one thing kept the manhunters riding westerly in this great emptiness: the tracks of horsemen. Even so, Will Stanton said aloud unless they found what they were looking for soon, they could end up riding into the very distant sunset and perhaps in time, ride all the way into eternity.

Arch smiled, scratched inside his shirt and

commented, 'We'll find 'em. With Quiroz unable to keep this up much longer, they got to stop.'

Stanton gestured with an up-flung arm. 'Where? You see a place they could stop?'

Arch didn't answer, he was more worried about the sun which was close to setting, dying altogether with dusk to follow. As good as the tracks were in this kind of country, to follow them after nightfall a man would just about have to do it down on all fours.

10

Tracks and a
Speckled Dog

Their attention as well as the attention of their
horses was abruptly caught by a shaggy black and
white dog running for its life with a mangy dog
coyote in panting pursuit.

Will laughed. 'He'll never catch her.'

Arch reined northward in the direction of the
chase and he neither spoke nor smiled until the dog
coyote saw horsemen behind him and gave up the
pursuit to race easterly until he disappeared in a shal-
low arroyo.

The black and white dog continued to run, occasionally looking back. Evidently her fear of the dog
coyote now included the pair of riders loping behind
her because she tucked tail and with her guard hairs
scraping the ground abruptly went over the side of
an arroyo and disappeared.

Arch and Will stopped on the arroyo's edge. The
bitch was still running but not as fast as she headed
straight for some unkempt old cottonwood trees and
an area of grass, underbrush and of all things, roses.

They slid down from the rim to the lower area. Their horses picked up the gait and they passed through a flourishing high thicket and emerged in a grassy place of about three or four acres in the middle of which, close to a bricked-up spring, stood a very old adobe. The dog was nowhere in sight but a man was. Not above average height, in fact a little less. His skin was dark, his hair was almost white. He didn't appear to be armed but as the men from Cold Spring approached Arch recognized the area around the man's middle which was lighter than other parts of his trousers. He wore a sidearm; he wore it often otherwise his britches would have been uniformly faded.

He neither smiled nor nodded as the strangers reined up a few feet away and Arch said good morning in Spanish, to which the dark man barely inclined his head.

He was not young, perhaps in his sixties, his eyes were very dark and hooded like the eyes of a harrier hawk.

He did not invite the strangers to alight, which was the custom. Neither did he speak for a long time but eventually he said, 'You are lost?'

Arch gazed thoughtfully at the older man. 'My name is Arch Trumbull,' he said. 'Constable at the Cold Spring settlement.'

This statement ordinarily encouraged a similar introduction but none was forthcoming until the dark man had finished his study of the horsemen, then all he said was, 'If you are looking for *mesteños*, there are none anywhere around this place.'

Will had been studying the house, which generations of inhabitants had added on to until the residence had about five or six rooms.

There was a brush corral north of the house, obviously for goats or sheep but it was empty except for a dozing horse under a ragged old tree.

The man spoke again, clearly but in a stilted way. 'I live alone.' He pointed. 'My wife is buried there.' As he lowered his arm he said, 'What is it that you want?'

Arch jutted his jaw Indian fashion. 'We've been following the tracks of three horses.'

The white-headed man looked, cleared his throat and said, 'I think those are from my horse, I ride out to hunt.'

Arch slowly wagged his head. '*Amigo*, those tracks were not made by that animal under the tree who has no shoes. Those tracks were made by shod horses, and they came this way, they did not go the other way.'

The older man shifted his gaze and seemed about to speak when another man appeared in the doorway, leaning against the door jamb. He wasn't smiling and the cocked six-gun in his right fist was as steady as stone when he said, 'I know you, Constable. I came back to kill you for scattering the horses. I had them sold in Mexico. They're waiting down there for them. I can't tell them there will be no horses. You understand?'

The older man moved slightly to one side so that the man in the doorway had an uninterrupted view of the pair of riders.

Arch leaned both hands atop the saddle horn. 'You'll be Frank Allende,' he said, and the man in the doorway's face had a momentary expression of annoyance. 'Pancho,' he said.

'*Comprehendo!* Pancho. Pancho Jefferson.'

Arch nodded, the names were inconsequential, the gun was. 'Pancho Jefferson.'

The man in the doorway's expression brightened. 'That's better. We need your horses, get down with both hands where I can see them.' As Will and Arch were dismounting Pancho Jefferson gave the old man an order. 'Go take their guns and bring them to me. *Viejo!* Not that way, to one side of them. Go!'

The older man neither spoke nor looked up as he came to the near side of the constable and his companion, disarmed them and obediently took their weapons to the doorway where he dropped them. This time when he faced around although his expression showed nothing his eyes spoke volumes.

The man in the doorway was neither tall nor fleshy. It was probable that not only his disposition but his way of life, constantly running, offered little opportunity for him to remain in one place long enough to eat well and often, made him brusque.

His clothing was stained, sweaty and a mixture of border Mex and *gringo*. He had as good a command of English as did the blue-eyed horsethief, but where Quiroz had almost no discernible accent Pancho What-ever-his-name was did have.

The old man grumbled. 'The meat is burning,' and Pancho tipped his cocked weapon signalling the old man to go inside.

Both the *gringos* were larger, strong men but a cocked Colt made its possessor ten feet tall and of unequated strength.

Will spoke for the first time. 'Where is Quiroz?'

'Inside.'

'How is his leg?'

Pancho sighed. 'We stopped here to find a buggy, there was none and the dog told us you were coming. I think if you hadn't followed her you wouldn't have found us.'

Stanton said, 'Mister, shod horses leave good sign. We'd have found you.'

Pancho's reply to that was quietly given. 'That's too bad, *gringo*. The old man can bury you after we are gone.'

Arch got the subject back where he wanted it. 'Make a travois,' he said, and the renegade sighed again. 'There is bleeding and one of the sticks is broke. Jesus is out of his head sometimes.'

'Leave him behind,' Arch suggested, and got an unwavering glare from the horsethief. 'You would do that,' he said. 'You *gringos* leave the injured behind. The Indians waited for you to do that, but in my family it's not done. That's why we need a buggy, even a wagon. All this old road runner has is a lazy old horse.'

Arch tried again. 'You know how the soldiers carry their wounded?'

'In hospital wagons. In Mexico they do the same. some of the time,' Pancho shrugged.

Arch's next remark ignored Pancho's innuendo. 'They make slings of blankets between two horses.'

Pancho considered this. 'Very quiet horses, then,' he said, and seemed to brighten. 'You know how this is done?'

'Yes.'

'Then you will do it.'

Arch looked steadily at the renegade. 'Be glad to, after you tell me somethin'. Why did you come back for Quiroz?'

'First, I came back to kill the man who spoiled our horse drive, secondly I came back because we could not find Jesus, only his horse. So we tracked where he was led to the village. So he didn't get killed on his horse, he was only hurt. Constable, there are a hundred tongues and a hundred ears. There are even more *ojos*. You understand? I knew where you took him. I didn't know it was only his leg until we came for him.'

The old Mexican came up to speak irritably to Pancho in Spanish. 'He is crazy in the head, he threshes about and he is bleeding.'

Pancho gestured with his six-gun. 'Whichever one of you fixed his leg go inside and do it again.'

Arch stood his ground. 'You didn't answer my question. Why did you risk coming for him?'

The loosely held Colt firmed up aiming low. Will held his breath watching the finger in the trigger guard. For several seconds the renegade and constable looked unwaveringly at each other before Pancho said, 'Three times he saved my life. It would mean nothing to a *gringo*. To me he is my brother. You don't understand that, do you?'

Arch didn't respond, he walked directly toward the outlaw, roughly shoved the six-gun aside and followed the old man inside.

There were six rooms. Originally there had been one. There were no windows and the walls were three feet thick to guarantee that summer or winter the interior temperature was always the same.

The house smelled of goats, it was not a tidy nor clean place. There were two candles burning on a table with benches where a meal had been inter-rupted. The black and white dog watched everything from her hiding place among some ancient blankets in a gloomy corner.

Will remained with the horses. He could have hobbled them but a man with rolled-up sleeves and blood-slippery hands appeared in the doorway. He made no move to draw his sidearm, he simply stood looking at Stanton. He had a lantern jaw, a hooked nose and small, very dark eyes set in a face the colour of old mahogany. He spat and dragged a soiled hand across his mouth. He said nothing, he did not have to, his look of hatred was sufficient.

The old man appeared, shouldered past the glaring renegade and told Will to take the animals to the empty corral and off-saddle them.

Jésus Quiroz was sweat drenched and wild-eyed. When Arch leaned to touch him, Quiroz spat curses in two languages. Arch looked at the leg; aside from the soiled bandage one of the splints protruded. As he straightened back Pancho said, 'Do something, *gringo!*'

Arch continued to look at the blue-eyed man when he replied, 'I'm not a doctor.'

'But you helped him before.'

Arch gestured. 'Hold him still. I'll take off the bandage.'

The suggestion was sound but Pancho had to call to both his Spanish-speaking companion and the old man before he could hold Quiroz for Arch to remove the bandage. What he saw would have destroyed any hunger he might have had. The wound was raw, the lower part of the splint was lodged in it, Quiroz was bleeding badly.

Arch pulled the splint loose and stopped the fresh flow of blood by using his belt above it and twisting it using the slippery splint. He looked at Pancho, whose expression was difficult to define. Arch asked if the old man had whiskey, pulque, tequila, anything at all, and the old man scuttled from the room. When he returned he didn't have a bottle he had an earthen jug. He handed it to Arch as he said, '*Tizwin.*'

Arch growled for the old man to tip Quiroz's head and told the others to restrain the injured man.

Arch had to use a finger to make Quiroz swallow and got several swallows of the Apache whiskey down, handed the jug back to the old man and shook his head. Quiroz had ingested about four swallows, usually no more than three were required to knock a man out. It was strictly forbidden for Indians to make *tizwin*, but the white-headed old man was not an Indian and the formula was very simple. Mostly, neither Mexicans nor *norteamericanos* would touch the stuff. It had a very bitter taste.

Quiroz eventually got limp and Arch called for Will Stanton.

Will stopped in the doorway where eight candles burned, and for a moment held his breath. He remembered butchering hogs, between those days and this day he had not seen so much blood.

Arch used *tizwin* for disinfectant. The room smelled powerfully of it. He asked if the old man had any clean cloth and again the adobe's owner scuttled away.

Arch showed Pancho how to manage the belt, to allow a trickle of blood now and then. Pancho nodded and leaned to hold the half a splint.

Arch and Will exchanged a look about the time the old man returned with two old and faded but clean shirts. The surly renegade told him to cut them into strips and the old man looked from his shirts to the mean renegade and went to work with a bone-handled clasp knife.

Pancho looked up from a sweat shiny face. 'What happens when the belt is no longer tight?'

Arch replied bluntly, 'The bleeding will start again. I don't know how much more he can lose.'

Pancho said, 'Sew it. I've seen them sew up horses.' He faced the old man. 'You have needles and thread?'

Before the old man could reply Will Stanton spoke. 'You sew it, mister, and it'll swell and bust the thread.'

Pancho looked fiercely at Stanton. 'You know what to do?'

Arch answered. 'Tie it with bandaging as tight as he can stand it. Make the bleeding stop.' Arch and the renegade looked steadily at each other over the unconscious man. 'You damned idiot,' Arch said quietly. 'You should have stopped when you saw the blood.'

'Where, *gringo, salao*? There was no place.'

Arch did not argue, he considered Quiroz's shiny face, gestured for Will to make a tight bandage over the wound while Arch held the leg up.

The old man crossed himself. When the others were concentrating on the bandaging he hoisted the jug with one arm in the bend of his shoulder and drank before stoppering the jug and placing it again on the earthen floor.

Quiroz groaned and Pancho glared at Stanton. 'You are killing him!'

Will straightened up and gestured. 'If you can do

better, do it,' and started to move away. Instantly Pancho's six-gun appeared. He cocked it. '*Gringo*, I'll kill you!'

Stanton was not cowed. 'Then who will finish?'

Arch leaned and struck Pancho's gun wrist. 'Put that damned thing away. *Do it*! *Now*!'

The gun slid back into its holster. Arch considered the bandage where blood was showing. He told Will to make it tighter and get the damned job finished.

The room was so quiet, the cry of a distant coyote sounded loud despite the thick walls, and the dog shot out the door. The old man profanely called her and she slunk through the door back to her bed and the old man explained. 'They will kill her. They killed three dogs for me.'

The vicious-looking renegade growled at the old man. 'Be quiet you old *bastardo*,' and the old man did not speak again.

It was getting cold with the door wide open. The old man went to close it and make a fire in his iron stove. He took the jug with him but the mean-eyed renegade told him to bring it back and leave it. Again the old man obeyed without a word before scuttling back to feed his stove.

No one had any idea how much time had passed until Arch lowered the rebandaged leg and stood watching for telltale blood, saw none and addressed Pancho What-ever-his-name-was.

'You can't move him.'

'We'll find a wagon.'

'Not even a hospital wagon,' Arch stated. 'Mister, if he pulls through it will be a miracle. He can't be moved for weeks, maybe months.'

Both renegades stared at Arch who ignored their

expressions of hostility, picked up the jug, swallowed twice and handed it to Will, who also swallowed twice. He did not offer the jug to the renegades, he stoppered it and put it on the floor, picked up some unused cloth and ignored everyone until he had wiped his hands then he addressed the vicious-looking renegade. 'You got a name?'

The renegade glared without replying but Pancho did. 'His name is José.'

Will tossed the rag aside, it had been a shirt sleeve. He gave the fierce-eyed outlaw look for look when he spoke again and brought his right hand from behind his back with a six-gun in it. 'Empty your holster, *bastardo*.'

They were no more than ten feet apart facing each other. Arch quietly said, 'You better do it, José. He'll blow your head off.'

The renegade still made no move to obey but when Pancho told him to obey he emptied his holster. Will made a wolfish smile. 'I picked it up on my way inside. Pancho. . . ?'

This time there was no delay, the gun made a solid sound as it struck the ground. Pancho was not intimidated. He ignored Will and the gun and addressed the constable.

'He will go with us.'

Arch shrugged. 'Fine. He saved your bacon. You said three times. Now you're goin' to let him die. He won't get a mile before the bleeding starts.'

Pancho looked down at the unconscious man, looked up and said, 'Constable, if he stays here you will bring the law.'

Arch leaned far back to ease the pain in his back from so much leaning. 'Leave him here an' he'll

maybe have a chance. I wouldn't bet a plugged
centavo on that, but if you move him. . . .' He leaned
to spring his back a second time.

The old man risked speaking without looking at
the killer who told him to be quiet. He said, 'I can
look after him,' and the lantern-jawed outlaw
snorted. 'You can't even clean your house, you old
goat,' he exclaimed scornfully.

Arch ignored them both and again addressed
Pancho. 'I'll fetch someone to look after him,' he
said, and the killer renegade turned on him.

'A hangman! Another policeman! I wouldn't trust
you for. . . .'

'*Silencio,*' Pancho said, and added more, also in
Spanish. 'Your mouth keep closed!'

Pancho faced Arch looking more frustrated than
angry. 'Whoever you bring, people will know. We stay
alive only by moving, never staying, always moving.'

Arch was tired and finally, his hunger returned.
'No one will know.' He looked at the old man who
immediately protested that he never left his arroyo,
hadn't been to a settlement in thirty years, would say
nothing, ever.

No one smiled but later Arch and Will Stanton
would. Pancho wanted to know who this person was,
'From the settlement? His family will wonder him
being gone so long. They will talk and. . . .'

'It's not a him,' Arch interrupted to say. 'It's a her,
an' she don't live in the settlement. Mister, take it or
leave it. Kill the man who saved your life or get on
your horse and leave, and take buckle-jaws with you.
Come back in two months, maybe then Jésus can ride
with you.'

11

The Constable's Idea

José growled at his *jefe* and got a snarled response. 'We will leave him! Go bring in the horses!'

After the lantern-jawed man had departed in sullen silence Pancho leaned, retrieved his belt-gun, holstered it and looked steadily at the constable. 'I tell you somethin,' he said quietly. 'When we come back, if he has died, I will find you and slit your throat.'

Arch knew sincerity when he heard it. 'I can't guarantee you he will live, but I can guarantee you we will do everything possible to see that he recovers.'

José appeared in the doorway to announce the horses were ready. He smelled strongly of grease-wood so the renegades had hidden their horses well.

Pancho looked at Quiroz for a long moment before telling the passed-out man in Spanish that he would return and that they would ride again. It was a promise not to be kept; no one had the right to suggest the coercion of a fate that neither sees nor hears such promises.

133

After the renegades were gone the old man hoisted his jug again. Arch took it away from him and growled to be fed. Hunger could be appeased but nothing short of quiet and relaxation could appease bone-weary tiredness.

They went outside to make certain their horses would have feed and water and while they were out there Arch leaned on the corral gazing northward.

As Stanton had done before, he guessed the constable's thoughts. 'If she will do it,' he said, and Arch turned slowly to regard the stockman. 'She will,' he said, and paused before also saying, 'José would have dragged Quiroz along.'

Stanton nodded. 'Somewhere down the line that son of a bitch is goin' to get killed, an' as far as I'm concerned the sooner the better.'

Arch nodded gently and returned to watching the horses. 'Pancho's harder to figure out. He'd kill at the blink of an eye, but he risked a lot to come back for Quiroz. Maybe there is honour among thieves after all.'

Stanton said nothing. He was having trouble keeping his eyes open. They returned to the *jacal* where the old man was frying meat and some unidentifiable vegetable that looked like asparagus and smelled like onions.

He had been at the jug during their absence and as a result was talkative. He told them many years ago he had been a *renegado*, an *apóstata*, that he had ridden with men like Pancho Allende, and others who were worse, that he had bribed a *rurale* after he was to be hanged, and had never returned to *Mejico*. He told them of his wife, and how much he missed her, that they had been married by a priest at a mission but that the Good Lord in His wisdom had refused them children because of the terrible things the old man had once done.

He even got an ancient, dusty and battered mandolin and while they were eating sang of broken hearts, lost love and death.

Before he finished, Will looked across the table at the constable, who shrugged. 'They always sing sad songs.'

Will sat with Quiroz until he could no longer keep his eyes open, then Arch did the same with an identical problem. The old man offered to sit with Quiroz. Will took the old man's weapons with him and bedded down with them beneath the smelly old blankets.

The old man could have stealthily retrieved the guns but kept his promise to sit with the wounded man, which he did until he heard snoring, then he systematically and without haste emptied Quiroz's pockets. He left the silver medallion on its chain around Quiroz's neck. He also left three or four silver coins. He was interested only in money and got a windfall he hadn't imagined.

Quiroz had a thin length of leather sewed on the backside of his pistol holster. The old man found it by accident.

He peeled off one corner very carefully, saw the greenbacks and was less careful peeling off the rest. The money was in US currency and was in a variety of large denominations the old man had never seen before.

He hadn't been sleepy before but afterwards he couldn't have slept and by dawn when Arch appeared in the doorway and Quiroz groaned, ground his teeth and opened his eyes the old man eagerly volunteered to make breakfast and left the room.

Quiroz's leg hurt less when it was not moved but he had a headache that showed no sign of abating. He and Arch talked, mostly the blue-eyed man listened, jaw cocked, fists clenched beneath the blankets.

When the constable had explained that Pancho had left after extracting a promise from Arch that Quiroz would be decently cared for until he was able to ride, the blue-eyed man's expression altered. He said he couldn't stay in this place and Arch told him he had no choice. He also told the outlaw he would bring a nurse to see that Quiroz did nothing to open the wound again, and this time the wounded man shot Arch a wary look.

'The nurse will tell people in the settlement. . . .'

'The nurse knows no one in the settlement and no one knows her.' Arch leaned to roughly brush Quiroz's shoulder before heading for the door. 'You will be safe.'

The horsethief said, 'How can I be safe? You are the law.'

Stanton called that the day's first meal was ready so Arch went to the doorway before also saying, 'In this place no one would find you, not even by accident. The law. . . ? That's my worry.'

'No,' Quiroz exclaimed. 'It is *my* worry.'

Arch turned. 'Only Will and I know you are here, and the old man. He told Allende he would say nothing. Neither will I nor Will.'

Quiroz stared. 'But you are the law. Why wouldn't you tell?'

Arch shrugged. 'I won't,' he said and left the room.

They ate in silence; the old man wasn't a bad cook except for the dried red peppers he seemed to put into everything, and for some reason neither the constable nor the stockman understood, the old man seemed to have shed twenty years; he smiled, he even laughed. He swore on his wife's grave he would take care of the horsethief.

An hour later when the men from Cold Spring were ahorseback, out of the hidden place and riding through sunlight, Stanton made a guess. 'The old man's alive, which he had no reason to believe he would be. I guess I'd sing and make music too.'

Arch said nothing. He was already losing interest in the old man, Pancho Whatever-his-name-was and the killer who had left with him.

Twice Will made an effort to recapitulate what had happened before giving up. He knew the constable was not a talkative man. On the ride back he was even less so.

They reached the settlement with the sun well down and soft shadows forming. Mary Elkins was waiting when Arch entered the store. 'Why don't you sell the store?' she demanded. 'You aren't by nature a storekeeper.'

Arch smiled in silence.

She said, 'You need a shave.'

He did not respond to that either. He left the store in search of Jim Meeker, who was out back forking feed to his trading stock. When Arch came out back the blacksmith leaned aside the hay fork and squinted. 'You'd ought to hear what folks are sayin'.'

Arch wanted to hire a saddle animal. Meeker stared. 'What's wrong with your horse?'

'He needs a rest.'

'All right. How long you need him?'

Arch couldn't even guess so he said, 'I'll pay you when I get back.'

Meeker's squint deepened. 'If you figure to go after them horsethieves, by now they're a hunnert miles deep in Chihuahua.'

Arch agreed. 'Maybe even deeper. I'm not goin' after 'em.'

Meeker's brow cleared. One of the rumours had to do with a female. There was a rumour that said the constable had been seen with a 'breed woman, but Jim Meeker knew better than to mention anything like that. He said, 'I'll fetch the horse.'

Arch told him to leave the animal tied out back, he'd be along for him directly, and that didn't make Jim wonder; he'd hired out other animals that riders didn't need until after supper.

Arch had to unlock the store's roadway door, Mary Elkins had locked it. He went through to his living-quarters, shaved, put several sticks of jerky in a pocket, ate some warmed over hash and went back through to lock the door from outside and walk southward through settling dusk. There were no people on the plankwalks.

The horse Meeker had left saddled was big, rawboned, with a jug head and small, piggy eyes. He wasn't young and had white hair at the withers but he was tough. It showed in a dozen ways.

Arch led him up the back alley, mounted near the north end of the settlement and rode parallel to the coach road for a mile. By then it was dark.

He did not expect to return to the settlement until morning, and that would only obtain if what he had in mind didn't pan out. If it did pan out he might not return to the settlement for possibly another day or two.

The jug-headed horse had a quirk. When Arch got off just shy of the Carlyle wagon tracks to pee, the horse stood, but when Arch turned to mount, had his left foot in the stirrup the horse flattened his ears and bared his teeth to bite.

It was a mistake, unquestionably it had worked other times but this time the fist that met his nose had enough power behind it to make the horse stagger a couple of steps.

That ended it. Arch and old jug head got along well, even when the horse scented-up other horses in the darkness and nickered. For this he got a slap alongside the jaw. He did not nicker again.

Where Arch left the road among the huge old trees moonlight was blotted out. He followed the path by instinct and memory, not by sight. When he saw pale light he loosened in the saddle.

When he was close enough he whistled twice so she was waiting, not in the doorway where light would limn her but to one side of the door with a Sharp's carbine in her hands.

He dismounted, nodded and led the horse to the shed, off-saddled it, hobbled it, draped the blanket and bridle from wooden pegs and turned. She was waiting with the old carbine held loosely. He said, 'I need a favour of you but first I'd admire some coffee.'

Without a word she took him to the house and inside where the lighted lamp softly glowed. There was an opened book on the table. She put the carbine back in its place across a set of antlers and went to poke wood into the cook stove.

There was a small fire burning in the fireplace. She told him to sit, which he did, and also dropped his hat on the floor. When she brought the cups of coffee and sat opposite him she said, 'What favour?'

He used no embellishment. 'There's a hurt feller in an old man's arroyo west of the settlement some miles. He needs care.'

'Who is he?'

Arch sipped coffee before speaking. This was the hard part.

'His name's Quiroz, he's one of the fellers who stole your pa's horses. He got shot when we turned 'em back. When he fell off his horse he also broke the same leg as got shot.'

She was expressionless when she said, 'One of my father's murderers?'

Arch shook his head. 'Not this one.'

'Why isn't he in the settlement jailhouse?'

'Well, the parson was lookin' after him up at his place when Quiroz's friends come in the night and took him away. He started bleedin'. They found the old man's place and took him there. They left. Will Stanton, that rancher who lost ten horses to the horsethieves, was with me. They wanted to take Quiroz with them. We rebandaged him. I told 'em if they moved him an' he started bleedin' again, he'd die. They left.' Arch leaned on the table. 'He needs a woman to look after him. The old man where he is now is dirty and useless at something like this.'

'You could find someone in the settlement, couldn't you?'

'Maybe, but if I did whoever went out there to look after him would return an' tell folks where she'd been an' why. You, they wouldn't know.'

Muriel Carlyle leaned back. 'Tell me one thing; why are you doing this?'

'I can't exactly explain, but if folks in the settlement find him they'll drag him to the nearest tree an' hang him.' Arch paused. 'We talked. He's an outlaw, has been for some years, but Muriel, he's not – well – he's different from outlaws I've known.'

She went to the stove to refill the cups and return with them. As she sat down she asked another question. 'Where is Will Stanton?'

Arch had no idea. 'Down in the village I expect.'

'You should have brought him with you. He might tell people what you two have been doing.'

That had been an oversight; Arch thought about it now. There was a good chance Stanton would bed down. They'd both been worn out when they got back to the settlement. He told her she could be right. He also told her he hadn't thought of Stanton after they left the outlaw, he had been thinking of her, wondering whether he had the right to ask her to get involved, also wondering if she would do as he asked.

She looked around the room with its comfort, its peacefulness and its highly prized seclusion. When she looked back she asked if it would be possible to bring the wounded outlaw to her log house.

He had already explained about the danger of moving Quiroz so he simply shook his head.

'For how long?' she asked.

He was bluntly truthful. 'At least four weeks. Maybe more like six weeks. He lost a lot of blood.'

'He's a horsethief, a renegade, maybe a killer. I don't understand why you are doing this?'

He leaned to retrieve his hat as he answered her. 'It's a feelin' I have. I don't know any better way to say it.'

He dropped the hat on and arose. 'I didn't have no right to ride up here tonight. Will an' I'll trade off lookin' after him.'

She waited until he was at the door before speaking. 'What will I need to bring along?'

He stopped with a hand on the latch. 'I don't know. I'll fetch medicine from the store.'

She arose. 'I'll get my coat and things.'

He watched her pass beyond a hanging drapery which served as a door and had misgivings. He called to her. 'No. I don't think you should do this. It might be dangerous.'

She called back. 'No more dangerous than having bears try to break into the house, and no more dangerous than having packs of wolves follow when I go after herbs and such like.' When she reappeared she was bundled into a sheep-pelt coat and had a holstered six-gun belt around her middle on one side and a large stag-handled fleshing knife in a beaded sheath on the other side.

She had what appeared to be a bedroll over one shoulder and had a booted carbine over the other shoulder.

He grinned. She handed him the bedroll at the door and looked up. 'I don't have a horse.'

'We'll make it on the one I'm riding. It'll likely take most of the night . . . Muriel?'

'I didn't imagine that would be why you come visiting, but if you put so much store in an outlaw. . . . Are you sure he wasn't one of 'em that killed my father?'

'The one that killed Abe was a born killer. This one's not.'

'What is he then? He steals horses and you said he's done other things.'

'He's helpless. There's a chance he won't make it. If you're askin' why I'm doin' this I'll say what I already told you – I don't know. It's somethin' I feel.'

12

An Almost Rainy Day

He was right about one thing, before they entered the arroyo from the north, cold air warned them that dawn was not distant.

When they'd cared for the jug-headed horse and Arch rattled the door, the old man opened it a crack and pushed a pistol barrel out. He swung the door wide, greeted the constable and stared at the woman. Arch told him her name was Muriel Carlyle. The old man said, 'I seen you once when you was a button.' He didn't say his name but led the way to the lighted room where Jésus Quiroz was smoking a foul-scented cigarette the old man had rolled for him. Except for dark places beneath the eyes and a burgeoning dark shadow of beard, he looked to Arch better than he had the last time they had met. He even gallantly inclined his head and smiled when Muriel was introduced to him. Except for his blue eyes and her dark eyes their colouring was close enough for them to pass as brother and sister.

Arch showed her the bandaged wound and was

gratified that no blood had seeped through. Without a word she draped her gun, shellbelt and coat from a wall peg. When she faced the bed she asked a question of the man in the bed. 'I'm the daughter of the old man you stole horses from. Who killed him?'

Quiroz's eyes widened. 'His daughter? The man who killed him was named José Sanchez.'

'There were two sets of tracks,' the woman said, without blinking.

'The other man was Pancho Allende who also calls himself Jefferson. But it was José who clubbed the old man.'

Muriel put her attention on Arch. 'You're right. I don't understand why you help this – this *bandolero*.'

Both men were silent until the old man appeared in the doorway. He was holding a dusty old bottle. He addressed the woman. 'I knew your father, well, we weren't exactly friends but I met him a few times when I was hunting.' The old man paused. 'The last time I had to walk nine miles without my britches.' He held up the bottle. 'Wine I made from wild berries. I'll get three glasses.'

Arch dryly said, 'Me'n the lady would like to be fed.'

The old man hesitated, he was disappointed. He only had four bottles of wine left. He kept them in a dark place that they shared with spiders.

He went to start a meal. Quiroz gestured Muriel toward a chair. She remained standing and while Arch had thought he'd come to know her, the woman at the foot of the bed wore a hard, almost hostile expression. Eventually she addressed Quiroz, 'I do this as a favour to the constable.'

Quiroz nodded again, sober and mildly troubled.

He asked Arch if Pancho and José had left his horse. Arch didn't know but he understood why the wounded man had asked and answered accordingly. 'You're not even goin' near a horse for a long time.'

The old man called. The meal he had prepared was sumptuous compared to meals the constable'd had lately. The old man had poured two glasses of red wine and hovered to see if his guests would drink. Eventually they did, and both smiled. The old man was delighted and showed it.

Dawn was breaking when Arch got astride the jug head and rode out of the arroyo. He was satisfied the outlaw would be competently cared for, not with warmth but with good care.

The sun was high when he reached the north-south coach road and went down it to the settlement. He veered easterly to the far-side alley and went down as far as Meeker's corral where he dismounted.

The blacksmith came out holding a thick mug of black coffee. He said, 'Four bits, Arch.' As the constable handed over the requisite half dollar Meeker said, 'You brought him back in good shape.' Because the remark annoyed him, Arch said, 'What did you expect?' and went up to the store, walked in and scowled. It worked; Mary Elkins did not say a word.

Three days later when he was considering riding to the arroyo, a hawk-eyed, greying man walked in, looked steadily at Arch and said, 'I'm US Marshal Tom Gorman. You'll be Constable Archibald Trumbull?'

Arch winced. No one had called him Archibald since he'd been large enough to teach them otherwise.

They briefly shook hands. The steely-eyed individual asked for, and got, a cigar which he took his time lighting before saying, 'I been lookin' for a feller named Will Stanton. I was told you two was friends. You seen Mister Stanton today?'

Arch hadn't. In fact he hadn't even thought about Will for a couple of days.

'Last I saw,' he told the federal lawman, 'was a few days ago.'

The federal officer savoured his stogie and spoke around it. 'If you see him I'd be right obliged if you'd tell him I'm lookin' for him. We got ten horses wearin' his brand the army bought sight unseen. The gov'ment sent word to the commandin' officer at Fort Buchanan to keep them horses corralled until Mister Stanton come for 'em.'

Arch loosened. 'He'll be glad to hear that, Marshal. I'll look him up. Where'll you be?'

'At the saloon. You might explain to Mister Stanton that it was the CO at Buchanan who wrote about them horses bein' stolen. He might want to thank the officer for gettin' them back for him.'

The settlement wasn't so large a man couldn't be found but the nearest thing the constable got to locating Stanton was when the parson told Arch he and the stockman had visited for a spell last evening, and Stanton had mentioned having to ride westerly to pay a visit. What they had talked about was the wounded outlaw being spirited out from under the parson's nose.

Arch had one question for the holy man. 'Did he say anything about where Quiroz and his friends might have gone?'

'He didn't know,' the preacher replied. 'We tried to figure that out and neither one of us could come up with an answer, but we both agreed moving Quiroz would likely result in him bleedin' to death.'

Arch was relieved. Muriel's notion of Stanton telling what he knew evidently hadn't happened.

Arch got his horse and with Mary Elkins scowling from in the doorway of the store as she watched him leave the settlement riding west, his relief was strong enough so that he watched birds take wing as he passed the tiny lavender flowers open wide toward the sun.

He knew he had guessed right as he skirted the arroyo's rim before descending and saw two horses in the faggot corral. One's back was sweat dark.

When the old man opened the door Arch stared. He had shaved, combed his hair and wore clean britches and a faded old shirt. As he stepped aside for Arch to enter he said, 'They get along famous, but it took a while. She's real handy.'

When the constable got to the bedroom doorway Muriel and Quiroz were playing stick poker. She looked around and smiled, something Arch hadn't seen her do in quite a spell. Quiroz nodded as he said, 'Her pa taught her poker. We been playin' for two days an' I ain't won a single hand.'

Will Stanton came in from outside. Arch took him to one side to explain about the federal marshal and his horses. Will wasted no time rigging out and riding out of the arroyo. The others asked no questions and Arch volunteered no information.

He stayed until the sun was low. Before leaving he took Muriel outside where they talked. On the ride back Arch shook his head. Her whole attitude had changed in a short period of time.

When he reached the settlement most of the

buildings were dark. Only the eatery and Joe Parker's water-hole showed lights. He went to the café and got a shock; Mary Elkins and Tim Farrel were dining at the only table. Farrel looked up and nodded but Mary Elkins raised her head, gave it an annoyed wag and went back to eating.

He visited the saloon and got another surprise, that steely-eyed federal officer and Will Stanton were trading off buying one another drinks. Joe Parker considered the constable and rolled his eyes. When Arch settled at the northernmost part of the bar Joe came along to lean and say, 'I don't know whether they got a bet laid or they're just tryin' to see who falls down first.'

Joe got Arch a bottle and glass and went down his bar where a red-faced Will Stanton poured silver coins atop the bar, jerked his head for the marshal to follow and walked out into the late evening .

Parker had his usual regulars who had been as interested as Parker was at the competitive drinking. As Arch tossed off his nightcap a loud noise rattled the front wall. The men looked around but did not move until Arch dropped a coin beside his glass, hitched at his britches and passed through the spindle doors. There wasn't a sound in the saloon, even Joe Parker, no longer wearing his arm in a sling but noticeably favouring it, seemed to have taken root.

Arch nearly fell when he stepped outside. Will Stanton was leaning against an empty tie rack grinning. The formidable US marshal was half on, half off the plankwalk. His hat was crunched flat beneath him. Will said, 'They come in all sizes. The bigger'n meaner lookin' they are the harder they fall. He's out like a light.'

Arch pulled the passed-out lawman out of the roadway, got him face up on the plankwalk and Jim Meeker happened along to help. As Jim straightened up from inspecting the federal lawman he said, 'Well, he can't spend the night here. Who is he?'

Stanton answered. 'US marshal out of Albuquerque, can't drink worth a damn.'

After speaking, Will groped for an upright post, gripped it and very slowly sank into a sitting position.

Meeker ignored Stanton and addressed the constable. 'The two of us can pack him down to my place. He can sleep it off in my haystack – for two bits.'

It was like carrying a sack of wet meal but they got him down there; they even worried hay aside to make him a comfortable place and left him. On the way back up through the smithy Meeker said, 'What'n hell is a federal marshal doin' here?'

Arch did not reply. When they came abreast of his store he went inside through darkness to his living-quarters and lighted a lamp. A garrulous voice said, 'Turn the damned thing down, it hurts my eyes.'

Arch looked at Will Stanton flat out on a wall bunk, crossed to the bunk, retrieved the stockman's hat from the floor and dropped it over his face. He then went to examine his alley door. It hadn't been locked. He made a mental note not to forget to lock it and shucked his boots, shellbelt, hat and without doing anything else crawled into the blankets of his bed.

Sleep was almost instantaneous. Except for the customary barking dogs the night was silent. There were high, storm clouds gathering which the constable did not know, in fact no one else in the settlement was aware until an hour or so before dawn those early risers with chores to do detected the smell without being able to see upwards.

By the time Arch rolled out, Will Stanton hadn't moved except to brush his hat aside. Arch shook Stanton, got a groan and left the stockman to finish sleeping it off and went out through the store, leaving it unlocked and headed for the eatery.

He had company; the counter was nearly full when the constable entered. A mountain of a gully-bearded man looked at the constable and in a growly voice said, 'There's talk up the line Cold Spring stood off a band of renegades drivin' stolen horses.'

Arch knew the large man, he was the only freighter who consistently hauled to Cold Spring. Arch was lighting into his breakfast when he replied.

'There's always talk. For a fact we did scatter a small band of Mex horsethieves.'

The bearded man's small tawny eyes remained fixed on the constable. 'Was one of 'em named Jefferson?'

Arch turned. The freighter came from the north, only went as far as Cold Spring then turned back. He asked where the freighter had heard that and got a direct, growly answer.

'From up yonder at a lay-by where freighters congregate. There was a feller named Burns; I've known him for years. He hauls east of Glorioso, risky business but he doubles the cost to make it worth it. He told me at our camp of this Messican called Jefferson.' The big man paused to briefly ruminate. 'You ever hear of a Messican named Jefferson?'

Arch paused to swallow before answering. 'His name's Pancho Allende.'

'Then why does he go by Jefferson?'

Arch shrugged as he reached for his coffee cup, and the bearded man said, 'It don't make no difference. He could call hisself Abraham Lincoln. He's dead.'

Arch's coffee cup stopped moving. 'Your friend who hauls down along the border told you that?'

'Yep. Seems this Jefferson or whatever-his-name-is, rode into a *rurale* ambush. Him an' another Messican, and got theirselves shot all to hell.'

Arch sipped coffee. The large bearded man arose, dropped coins beside his empty platter, nodded and walked out. He nearly collided with someone coming in. They both grumbled apologies before the freighter sidestepped aside and Will Stanton entered.

His eyes looked wet, he hadn't washed and as he eased down beside the constable he audibly groaned. The much experienced caféman brought Stanton a mug of black coffee and departed.

Arch relayed what the freighter had said and Will reached for the coffee without comment.

They left the eatery together. Will felt better but did not look better. He breathed deeply, mopped his eyes and asked about the federal lawman. Arch could only say what he and Jim Meeker had done the previous night.

Stanton finished wiping his eyes as he said, 'I knew he couldn't do it. Them rough-lookin', hard-actin' ones never can. They just think they can.' Stanton paused. 'I'm goin' down to that soldier fort, get my horses an' head for home.' He pushed out a hand. As they shook Trumbull said, 'I'm obliged for your help. I couldn't have done it otherwise.'

Stanton forced a weak smile. 'You take care. Mind that damned renegade you cottoned to. When I get home I'll write you a letter.'

They parted like that and Arch never received a letter from the stockman.

Mary Elkins came down with the grippe so he had to tend the store for almost two full weeks before she was able to mind things while he left the settlement riding westerly.

There were things to ponder as he let the animal slog along on a loose rein. Once his thoughts were interrupted by a raindrop on the hand. He looked up; the storm clouds were bearing south-westerly, which meant when the storm let go it would be some-where in the vicinity of Glorioso.

When he reached the arroyo the corral was empty, and that worried him until he got into the yard and hit the door with a fist. He hit it twice before the old man appeared, not from inside but from around the north side of his house.

He gave the constable no chance to speak first, he said, 'They're gone. Bought my horse and with him astraddle an' her walkin', they went in the direction of the Carlyle place.'

Arch dismounted. 'He wasn't in any condition to ride.'

The old man did not deny that. He said, 'It happened between me'n my wife pretty much in the same way. He told her he was ready. She told him he warn't ready. He got out of bed and gimped around until she told him if they tried it he could die, an' you know what he said to her? He said he wasn't afraid of dyin' an' if it had to come to that he wanted her to be with him. So they bought my horse an' struck out.'

Arch said, 'They'll never make it. He sure as hell won't,' and the old man offered a stout contradiction. 'Mister, they'll make it. It may take 'em a week of restin' now'n then, but them two'll make it.' The old man got his sly expression. 'They said for me to tell you, if you come out again, that they'd take it as somethin' special if you'd ride up'n visit 'em.'

Arch's horse yanked impatiently on the reins the constable was holding. He said, 'Hold still!' and returned his attention on the old man. 'Those Messicans that brought him to your place got killed in an ambush by *rurales* below the line.'

The old man smiled and spat. 'Good riddance. It troubled me that they might come back for the hurt one, specially that lantern-jawed son of a bitch.'

Arch considered the horse, which was now standing hip shot with both eyes closed. He would of course ride up yonder, when he could. As he turned to swing astride the old man made a final comment.

'Mister, I'd say them two come as close to makin' a match as you'll ever come across. I ain't no authority but I been through it, she's buried yonder. They put me in mind of us forty years back.'

Arch left the arroyo for the last time although he didn't know it, took his time returning to the settlement and after caring for his animal entered the store from out back and startled Mary Elkins and Tim Farrel. The cowman said nothing he was both surprised and embarrassed, but Mary Elkins did. She said, 'You forgot where the roadway door is? How long'll you be around this time? There was a federal marshal lookin' for you. I said there was no way of sayin' when you'd be back, the way things been goin' lately. He said for me to tell you he was right obliged, and left.'

Tim Farrel quietly and unobtrusively left the store. He remained out there until Mary Elkins came out carrying her purse. He followed her all the way to her house and up on to the porch before she acknowledged him, then she said, 'I don't want to wash no more dirty socks nor put a man to bed when he's throwin' up drunk. I'm too old to go through all that newlywed business again. For the last time, Tim, *no!*'

This time when she closed the door on him the cowman went straight to Joe Parker's place to loudly proclaim he would never again try to court a female woman who had as independent a disposition as a hog on ice.

Joe served him while wryly looking over Farrel. He didn't say it aloud but he thought it. Until next time. Young bucks in the rut were obnoxious enough, but they couldn't hold a candle to old ones.